I0685422

Books in

The Human-Hybrid Project

series:

Shattered by Glass

Inside the Darkness

The Mirror Cracks

Reflections of the Silverback

The Glass Siege

Taking the Tower

The Rage

Sunchaser's Gambit

The Electrified Sword

The Russian's Revenge

Taking
the
Tower

Taking the Tower

Farley L. Dunn

🍳🍳🍳 THREE SKILLET

Taking the Tower

Copyright © 2021 by Farley L. Dunn

1st ed.

Book 6 in the Series:
THE HUMAN-HYBRID PROJECT

This book may not be reproduced in whole or in part, by electronic process or any other means, without written permission of the publisher.

All Rights Reserved

Published in Fort Worth, Texas

 THREE SKILLET

www.ThreeSkilletPublishing.com

Three Skillet Publishing
PO Box 162194
Fort Worth, Texas 76161

ISBN: 978-1-957173-00-9

Printed in the USA

Taking the Tower

— Book 6 —

The Human-Hybrid Project

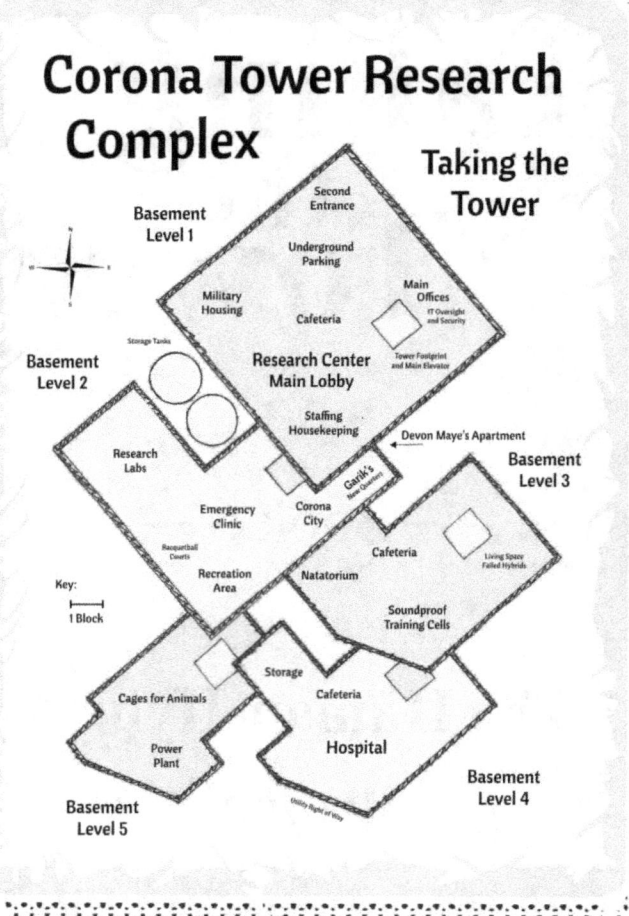

Corona Tower Research Complex

Taking the Tower

Basement Level 1

Second Entrance

Underground Parking

Military Housing

Cafeteria

Main Offices
IT Oversight and Security

Storage Tanks

Research Center Main Lobby

Tower Footprint and Main Elevator

Basement Level 2

Research Labs

Staffing Housekeeping

Devon Maye's Apartment

Garik's New Quarters

Basement Level 3

Emergency Clinic

Corona City

Cafeteria

Living Space Failed Hybrids

Racquetball Courts

Recreation Area

Natatorium

Soundproof Training Cells

Key:
1 Block

Cages for Animals

Storage

Cafeteria

Power Plant

Hospital

Basement Level 4

Utility Right of Way

Basement Level 5

Bay City
Uptown East Side

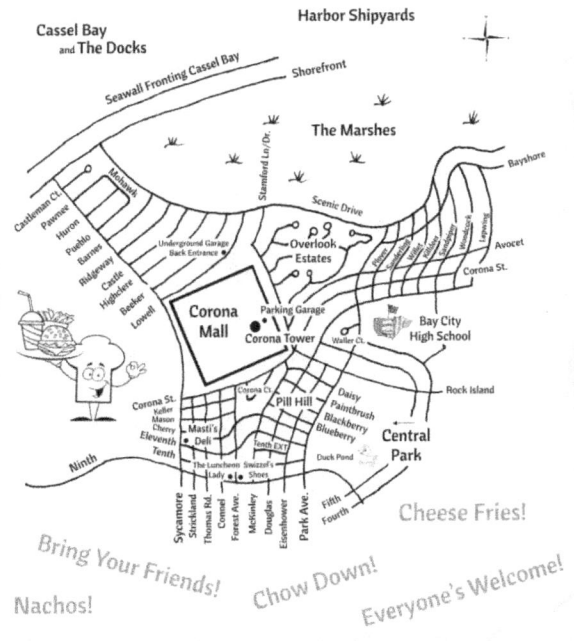

Cassel Bay
and The Docks

Harbor Shipyards

Seawall Fronting Cassel Bay

Shorefront

The Marshes

Castleman Ct.
Pawnee
Huron
Pueblo
Barnes
Ridgeway
Castle
Highbere
Becker
Lowell

Mohawk

Stanford Ln./Dr.

Scenic Drive

Bayshore

Overlook
Estates

Underground Garage
Back Entrance

Avocet

Corona St.

Corona
Mall

Parking Garage

Corona Tower

Waller Ct.

Bay City
High School

Rock Island

Corona St.
Keller
Mason
Cherry
Eleventh
Tenth

Corona Ct.

Pill Hill

Daisy
Paintbrush
Blackberry
Blueberry

Masti's
Deli

Tenth EXT

Central
Park

Ninth

The Luncheon
Lady

Swizzel's
Shoes

Duck Pond

Sycamore
Strickland
Thomas Rd.
Conmel
Forest Ave.
McKinley
Douglas
Eisenhower
Park Ave.
Fifth
Fourth

Cheese Fries!

Bring Your Friends!

Chow Down!

Everyone's Welcome!

Nachos!

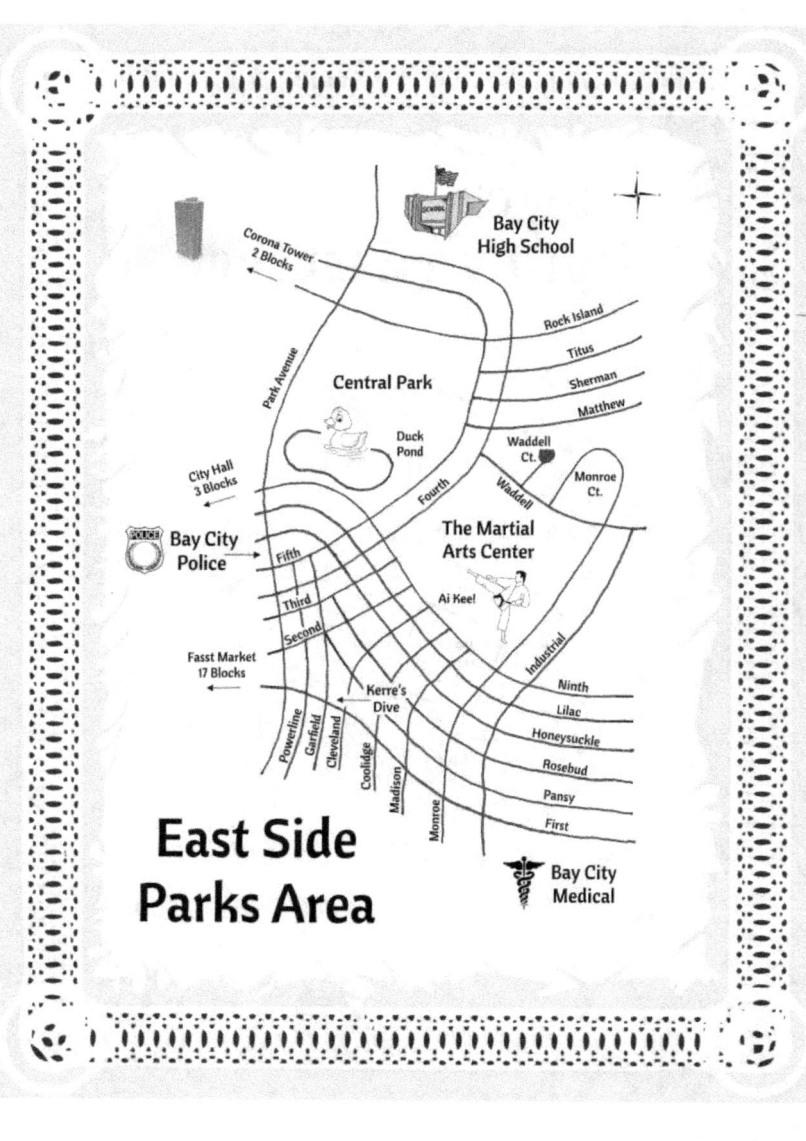

East Side
Parks Area

Bay City
Old Town East Side

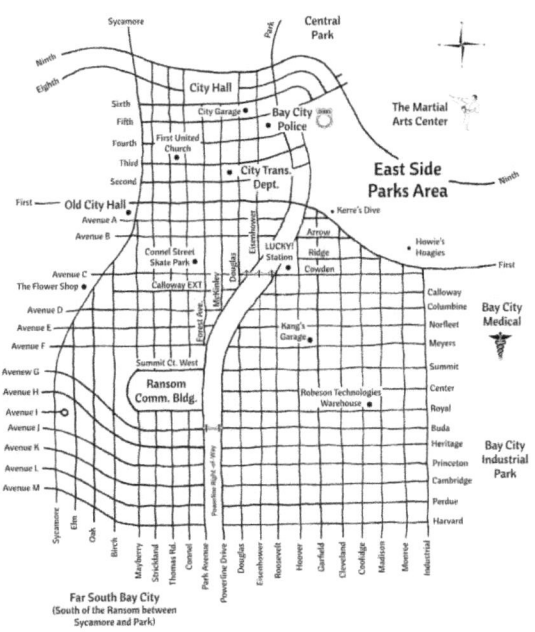

— I —

larms battered the Corona Tower security center.

Garik Shayk scanned the viewscreens covering the enormous wall in front of him. They towered five high and thirty or more wide, a kaleidoscope of moving shapes and repeating images that monitored the basement complex, the 40-story Tower aboveground, and anywhere in Bay City that cameras could be accessed.

Six months earlier, Corona Tower had been a fascinating draw to 17-year-old Garik, an object of desire for the rich lifestyle and the exclusivity that oozed from the shimmering glass building. It cut into the skyline, a black fist that dominated Bay City.

Then, he had fallen into the Tower's highly restricted basement research center and been forcibly inducted into the complex's military-funded human-hybrid research project. His girlfriend Marisa had managed to escape, but the trap had ensnared Garik, his DNA combined with that of a timber wolf and fed back into his veins.

Now, across many of the screens, people carried placards in the streets and smoke billowed from burning cars. Farther from the Tower, traffic moved along First or Sycamore, blissful drivers unaware of the gathering storm in Uptown. Inside the Tower, diners in the up-scale Stamford Suites Grill were insulated from the mayhem more than five stories below. Were they aware that the haze now filling the air wasn't rush-hour pollution but the bomb-strewn remains of the Corona Tower Parking Garage on the back side of the building? Would they care if they did?

A handful of the screens were blank, revealing camera feeds already lost. Garik had watched a protestor fling a brick at one, killing the image feed, and another had broadcast the bomb destruction in the parking garage before that camera, too, had winked out.

"We have a situation at Stamford and Avocet."

Garik searched for the speaker to his left. The words

had been whispered into a microphone, but his hearing was sharper than most, one bonus of his timber wolf DNA. He caught the acrid odor of restrained panic—again a byproduct of his enhanced DNA—and he located the speaker. She watched the wall of monitors, and he followed her eyes to a rough-looking crowd cheering and rejoicing. He cringed to see his face on a flag one of the revelers carried. Another turned to grab a brick—hefting it to check its throwing distance—and Garik's face rippled across the back of the man's shirt.

Not my fault, he thought, wishing the images away. He didn't want to be blamed for this, and Weston Rodheimer, the Director over the human-hybrid project, had already aimed a massive finger at him.

In the display, a military vehicle pulled up, and several suited individuals rolled out wearing masked riot gear with weapons in hand and began shouting instructions at the group. Trash and rocks flew, the man's brick hit the vehicle's windshield, people ducked, and the situation devolved into bedlam. Someone on the other side of the room overrode a third of the screens, calling out, "Eyes up. We have a runner." A handful of screens changed at once, revealing a drone view.

Garik followed the runner. Several goons gave chase, clumsy in comparison to the slim, female figure. The images on the screens shifted from drone to stationary cameras as buildings or trees obstructed the view. In the background, the duck pond in Central Park reflected the sky. The park was littered with tents and debris from protesters bused in from Oregon and Nevada. Tracking down Park Avenue for several blocks, with the runner and her pursuers leaping over tumbled trash cans and once dodging a car at an intersection, they passed the monument in the small park across from the police department.

Garik cheered the runner on, despite his frustration at the damage in the city being blamed on him. The runner dodged into an alley between Second and Third Streets, confusing her pursuers. The cameras searched for a moment before locating her on Eisenhower. The view shifted as the feed reset, and at the last moment, the runner turned and lobbed something at the goons, creating a flash-bang that washed out the video image. When the screens came back up, the goons held their arms over their face masks, and the runner was gone.

Garik had seen, though. The face, the lithe body, the running style. The runner was Marisa, his girlfriend before he was drafted into the DNA-enhanced human-hybrid shapeshifting project. An avalanche of memories swept away the room, and he was watching the stars with her on the roof of their apartment building, offering her a ride on his Street Strider, enjoying a snack with her on the Corona Mall and listening to her dreams of wanting to be this, do that, make something of her life.

He turned and ran from the maelstrom on the viewscreens. He thought he heard Lt. Col. Fair call his name, but he didn't slow down. Someone must have answers, and he wasn't finding them in that room.

LIFE at the main elevator block sucked the urgency from Garik's frantic run with soft lighting, scented air, and a cleaning lady whose name he didn't know running a floor buffer in a side corridor. He had expected a torrent of military types racing to reach the mall level and miraculously rebuild the entrance to the parking garage. A military contingent was assigned a large section of Basement Level 1, and they claimed a section of the underground parking garage for military only. Their entrance and exit? The bombed garage on Stamford.

Two researchers exited the elevator when the doors opened, pushing a cart loaded with computer equipment. They had to steady a loose monitor twice. They apologized, and irritated, Garik stepped through the door and inserted his passkey. Basement Levels 2 through 4 lighted, the only floors his key allowed him to visit. Not the mall, not the Tower's main lobby, and certainly not the upper floors of the 40-story Tower. He was just lowly Garik, peon research subject, too unimportant and too human to be trusted.

He touched Basement Level 2 for home. Kevin Lee, the acting activities director and Garik's "handler" was in a training session with Paul Gberie, who had been DNA merged with an octopus, giving him the ability to morph his skin color and texture to become essentially invisible. Paul's training was intended to teach him group cooperation and teamwork, and that meant Kevin was overseeing a soccer game.

Devon Maye, Garik's backup handler, should be in the apartment he and Garik shared. Devon had been injured in a car accident, and one leg sported a cast from thigh to foot, the reason Kevin had taken over the position of activities director.

The elevator dinged, and the door opened. Exiting, Garik caught his reflection in the mirrored ceiling. He had ridden this elevator with Marisa to the bottom floor of the basement using Halo Sunchaser's stolen passkey. Marisa had escaped. At least he could take some comfort in that. In the reflection, his hair now curled at his temples, and he looked very much like himself, unlike his shaved scalp from six months ago. The door dinged again, telling him it intended to close, and he retrieved his passkey and stepped into the corridor. He turned left toward Corona City and inserted the passkey that opened the door to the apartment.

"Hey, kiddo. Back already?" Devon had his leg propped on the coffee table with his tablet in his lap. Beside him, Annie Vanschooneveld, wearing red lipstick and her face softened by long bangs, leaned against him.

"I, um—" Garik hesitated. He'd wanted advice, someone to listen to him, to be able to vent his anger and frustration. Now, here, the normalcy of the room mired him in indecision. "I . . . there's a thing happening. I don't know what to do."

"That's odd." Devon, boyish with a blond cowlick at his temple, turned to Annie and winked. "He's never admitted that before. He always has all the answers."

Annie sat up. "What's wrong? Anything we can help you with?"

"The, um—" He looked behind him, realized he hadn't released the door to close, and he turned it loose, waiting until it latched. "You have Internet on that." The tablet, he meant.

"Of course."

Garik wasn't officially allowed access, but Kevin had made it clear his job confidentiality agreement only precluded him revealing what went on in the basement research center and not the other way around. Devon had resigned himself to going along and sharing what Garik wanted to know.

"Devon," Annie cautioned. "I hope you don't intend to do what I think he's asking of you."

Devon shrugged. "Too late. Kevin started it while I was still in the hospital and what was I to do? Anyway, I never let him touch it. I'm not that ready to lose my job." He nodded to Garik. "What is it you want to know?"

"Not me. I know all about it. You're the one who needs to know—"

"Wait a minute." Devon cut in with a puzzled look. "You are supposed to be with Kevin at Paul's soccer game. He sent you back on your own?"

"Just check the tablet. On the way to the game, Rodheimer and two goons commandeered me. Now everything's blown up. Literally. Use that and see if you don't believe me."

"Devon?" Annie reached for the tablet. "Let me see that. I knew things in the city were tense when I arrived this morning. There might be something to what he's saying."

Might be? Garik would have laughed if he weren't so stressed. Marisa! Running from the Tower's goons! Nobody down here concerned! And the parking garage collapsed, possibly all of it!

Then there was Rodheimer's threat against The Flower Shop, Colonel Brace intimating he would take control, and Rodheimer blaming it all on him. He would throw up, if it would help, but he suspected his stomach would still be an iron cable tied in knots.

Annie handed Devon the tablet as she glanced at Garik and back to Devon. Devon studied the screen, stroked the tablet several times, read something, then stroked it again. Without looking up, he motioned to Garik and patted the arm of the couch.

Garik found Annie had pulled up more than the

Tower's security cameras had shown. Bay City's news outlets were out in force, and they were having a heyday with the tsunami of violence sweeping across the city.

"Wow, kiddo." Devon shook his head. "The Director likes things to be as low-key as possible, and this isn't it."

"Not the Tower. That he likes to show off." Annie smiled and patted his arm. "I've seen the light show, and so has the city. Every night." Visual effects made it appear the obsidian glass tower repeatedly shattered into black glitter and showered the surrounding mall before reforming to do it all over again. It was the Tower's calling card.

"Right-o, but this is more. This involves the research down here in the basements, and the city doesn't know anything about that." He enlarged an image to reveal Garik's picture on clothing and banners. Several placards mentioned him by name, pleading with the Tower to relinquish the stolen child of the city. "I bet the Director will pull out all stops to get this under control. Not to worry."

"He can't. No one can get out, not any vehicles, anyway. The exit through the parking garage has been bombed."

Devon and Annie looked at each other, and Devon blew out his cheeks and released the air.

"Likely that's not going to be a problem," Devon

said, shifting uncomfortably on the couch and restricted in his efforts by his leg.

"Are you sure you should do this, Devon?" Annie's fingers fumbled with a button on her shirt, a clear sign she didn't think he should.

"What?" Garik wanted to say, *Just tell me!*

"There's something no one's shared with you . . ."

arik didn't get an immediate answer. Annie's watch chimed at her, and she glanced at it, sat up straighter, and apologized. "Excuse me. I must take this. Do you mind?"

"If you need privacy." Devon pointed to his bedroom.

"Oh, no. Not the bedroom." She laughed and winked at Garik, patted Devon on his good leg, stood, and walked past the front door into the darkened room.

She left the door open, letting the murmur of her voice as she answered the call filter back in.

Garik waited a moment for the promised revelation about the "something" that no one had told him, but the moment with the parking garage was broken, and Devon held out his hand.

"Help me stand, okay, kiddo?" He grinned awkwardly, as though he was intentionally shifting the conversation a new direction.

"Sure, Dev-o, change the topic. Leave me hanging." Garik grasped his hand and pulled, surprised at how light the tall man seemed. "Your crutches are right there."

"Hand them to me, please." Devon balanced easily using his good leg and his "mummy" one, but to walk was another matter.

Annie returned, slipping her sleeve down to cover her watch, and she hung a leather satchel over her shoulder. "My exit point. Sorry."

"You just got here." Devon's face fell. "Can't they give you even one morning off?"

"Not with what's going on upstairs. We've got partners across the globe calling in. News travels, and this more than some. I've got fires to put out and funding to save." She stepped to Garik and placed her hand on his forearm. "Devon thinks highly of you. If he gets crotchety, ignore him. The love is still there. I'm telling you this, because I don't think any of this is your fault. However, your name is at the center of the protesters' demands. That's not fair to you, and I know it. I don't know that I can insulate you, so prepare yourself. This isn't likely to be pretty."

She turned to Devon, blew him a kiss, and said, "Maybe next month, if this is all still here. What'cha say?"

"Right-o. What else can I say?" His shoulders sagged.

Annie laughed. She tossed her head slightly to one side to shift her bangs, stepped to the door and was surprised to find it locked. She dug in her purse and inserted her passkey. When the door unlocked, thump, thump, she questioned Devon, "Why is the door locked from the inside?"

Garik raised a hand.

"Oh, right. The jailbreak." She winked at Garik, slipped outside, and let the door close after her.

"SO, WHAT has no one bothered to tell me?" Garik followed Devon through his bedroom and into his bathroom.

"I shouldn't have mentioned that." In the bathroom, the blond man rested the crutches against the wall and stared at his face in the mirror. "You know I'm just an employee here, and right now, I'm not even a functional one, an amputee, almost." He pulled a washcloth from under the sink, flipped on the water, and soaked it.

He squeezed out some of the water, pressed the cloth to his face, and ran it over the back of his neck before dropping it in the sink. He pulled the towel from the wall and shook it out.

"Now," and Devon rubbed his face vigorously, leaving his shirt ringed with wet around the collar, "maybe I can think. You need an answer. In situations like this, I ask myself what Kevin would do."

"What's Kevin got to do with this?" Garik was out of patience, and he growled as he abandoned Devon for the living room. *Like always, don't tell Garik anything. Keep him in the dark.*

"I told you I was coming up with an answer. You don't have to be irritated." Devon followed on his crutches in his awkward three-legged gait.

"What gave it away? My hackles on end? Or maybe my howl of despair?" Garik stood at the real window opening into the corridor. The blinds were cracked, and outside, life continued as usual, busy in this part of Corona City. A man rode by on a Segway, a cloth backpack over his shoulders, and his hair in a bun. A pair of women shared a two-seater bike, the first one Garik had seen in the basement complex.

"Well, you did growl." Devon made it a joke. "Hey, kiddo, give me a break. I'm trying to think like Kevin. I can't just *tell* you, so, how can I tell you without actually telling you?"

"By just telling me?" Duh. How simple was it?

"Sorry. I'm not good at bending the rules like him. When I do, this happens." He tapped his plaster-encased leg. "Okay, I have an idea."

"Finally? The city is on fire, and it takes you this long?" Garik was surprised steam wasn't rising from his ears.

"Easy, kiddo. I'm not your enemy." Devon gathered the tablet, made his way to the table, and motioned for the teen to join him. "Let's have a geography lesson," and he tapped the screen to bring up a maps app.

"You do know stuff is blowing up in the city?"

"Back to the geography lesson. Humor me, okay? I'm trying to tell you what people haven't told you, and I'm trying to find a way to do it. Can we do this?"

"Why not?" No Dev-o this time. No teasing. No thump on the shoulder. Garik churned with impatience and irritation, and he wished Kevin were here. He at least told him stuff or said he couldn't, plain as that.

"This is Bay City from space." The water and the land split the image in two. Devon touched the screen, and the coastline expanded to reveal streets and buildings. None were identifiable, but Corona Mall, surrounding the Tower and covering 64 city blocks, was obvious, even from a distance.

"I know all this. What's your point?" Even irritated, Garik was curious if this was a live view and if he would see the smoke rising from the bomb blast that had taken down part of the Corona Tower Parking

Garage.

"The buildings." Devon shifted the image to a three-dimensional view, and as he zoomed in closer, it was clear it was still summer. Trees were in leaf, and yards popped with green.

"That's Overlook Estates. I can see the marsh, so that must be Scenic Drive. I don't see the Tower, but that's the north side of the mall. I've never been on some of these streets. That, though, is Lowell, and maybe that's Beeker Street next to it." Garik pointed to a street that took a sharp right for no good reason. "There Stamford Drive becomes Stamford Lane."

"I need you to look at the buildings."

Garik studied the image. From an overhead view, it had been difficult to see how the ground dropped off as it fell towards The Docks and Harbor Shipyards. In 3-D mode, it was easier. Corona Mall, while level across its surface, formed a cliff face of decorative stone and landscaping on the edge abutting Lowell. Past Lowell and Beeker, the app labeled the streets, Highclere, Castle, Ridgeway, all the way to Shorefront six blocks farther down. Each one dropped off, terraced and shadowed in the app's image.

After a short time, one building stood out. "That one." He pointed to a nondescript building fronting Lowell. It didn't reach the height of the mall's decorative cliff face so had a landlocked view, and tall landscaping crowded it on both sides.

"That one. Okay." Devon zoomed in closer. "What about it?"

"Can I?" He reached toward the tablet.

"Sure. Just no searches."

"Dev-o, I'm not stupid-o."

"I didn't say you were, just no searches." Devon set the tablet in front of Garik and released it.

Garik expanded the image again, shifted it so he could view the sides of the building, and noticed that parts of the building wouldn't come into focus, especially one end. The concrete parking lot in the front was also unusual. It was striped as if for parking, yet it was empty and looked as if it had never been used. Also, the lot simply blended into the street, except for a bold paint stripe where the curb should be, as if to allow access to larger-than-normal vehicles.

Two final things: The windows looked flat, like they were painted, and he couldn't find any air conditioning units to service the building.

"That's not a real building." Garik pushed the tablet away.

Devon studied the image. "Interesting. Now, tell me why there would be a building right there that's not a real building."

"So, you admit it? It's not real?"

"I'm not admitting anything. You said it, not me. I want you to tell me why there would be a fake building next to the mall."

"It's not tall enough to see in the mall—"

Devon nodded in approval.

"—and you can't see it from the mall."

Another nod, and a hand motion to continue.

"Landscaping hides most of it, and someone's gone to a lot of trouble to blur part of the picture. They want to hide something."

"Anything else?" Devon seemed pleased.

"No windows ... a dead giveaway—" causing Devon to pull the tablet to him to study it closer, "—and it doesn't have any air conditioners on the roof. It would be unusable in summer."

"I never noticed the windows. That's good. So, draw a conclusion."

"You're as bad as Jantzen." Garik rapped the table hard and looked away. "I always have to figure things out. Sometimes I can't."

"Okay, let me show you this." Devon tapped on the tablet, and he pulled up images of military vehicles all over parts of Bay City. There was no shortage. "These are current and dated from this morning. You can see the protesters. Even there, The Docks. How can they be there if the parking garage access is damaged? That's what I'm asking you to figure out." He said figure out with an emphasis to get Garik's attention.

An epiphany like bricks falling from the sky tumbled over Garik. The restricted underground parking garage, the vast number of military vehicles located there, the ramp leading up to the real world . . . most of those vehicles wouldn't be able to navigate the exit ramp, anyway. It was obvious. There had to be a back entrance.

"That building's the second entrance, isn't it?"

"I never said that." Devon smirked, pleased.

"Rodheimer said the city doesn't know about this research facility. There had to be a second entrance. It's the only way to move equipment in and out without anyone knowing." Garik imagined how it might work. The blurred end of the building as a massive garage door? Use the exposed parking lot as a lift, raising and lowering vehicles directly underground? He was certain there was a passage running underneath Lowell connecting directly with the parking garage underneath Corona Mall. How had he not already thought this possible?

"You shouldn't tell anyone you've figured this out.'

"I figured it out?" Garik barked a laugh. "You showed me."

"I will never admit to that." Devon held up one hand in a pledge. "I always suspected the entrance was on Lowell but wasn't sure. I mean, it had to be, didn't it? And that building? Now that I see it, of course."

"You didn't know?" Garik laughed, this time real. "All that, and you had no idea?"

"I just hadn't determined which building. I'm an employee. They don't tell us anything."

"Clearly."

"How could they make that building work as an exit? I've been up and down Lowell. It looks pretty normal."

"Maybe the exit's on the back side. I'm pretty sure the bushes on the side drop into the ground, like the entrance to Batman's lair," Garik teased.

"Could be." Devon tapped the tablet, bringing back the map. "Let me see if I can tell . . ."

Garik was more concerned about the images he'd seen on the screens upstairs. Marisa, running from the Tower's goons in their helmeted riot gear. What had she done for them to make such a fuss?

And that thing she threw, a flashbang grenade. Where had she gotten that? The questions kept coming, and none of the answers wanted to fall into place.

— 3 —

ven during the city-wide protests, the planned Friday-night events on the mall had taken place as scheduled. The perennial crowd favorite, the Dactyls, had performed two weekends in one month. A martial arts showcase—more martial than arts by the time it wound down long after midnight—had filled another weekend and decorated the pavers with copious amounts of Friday-night blood. Finally, Stephen Klandermans had volunteered to take on all comers in a wrestling competition, the challenge being that losers had to take a hit from another hybrid of their choice. Crowd participation was over the top.

That changed with the explosion that brought down a sizable portion of the aboveground two-story parking garage on Stamford. An announcement went out over the inhouse net that the week's entertainment would be postponed. The Tower's sign posted the news to Bay City as "necessary upgrades to prepare for the best spring season of new performance acts ever seen in Bay City history!"

The human hybrids that depended on their nights on the mall to let loose their inner fires and burn through their pent-up angst simmered. The first of the burning coals lobbed by the frustrated hybrids slammed into Garik and Devon the next morning as they made their way to the Level 1 cafeteria for breakfast.

Devon, still on his crutches, was determined to make a show of being able to get around, and entering the elevator, they were joined by three hybrids whom Garik recognized from his time in the recreation area and the gaming center. Fabiola Bello, a thick-bodied girl with a muscular stance and spiky blonde hair, took her place at the rear, flipping her thumbs back and forth with one foot against the wall. Raphaël Giannotti seemed planted to the floor, with tree-trunk legs and a gray cast to his skin. His nose required more real estate than his face seemed anxious to give. Finally, Mike

Lamonte, with tousled hair and large eyes that looked as though he could see everything around him without turning his head.

"Fabi, Raphaël, Mike." Devon greeted each one.

Garik nodded at the three. They weren't on Kevin's training schedule, so he hadn't interacted with them. He jotted their names on an internal list for future reference, picturing Fabi as a fighter, Raphaël as one of God's angels, and Mike saying, "Take a hike!" certain he would remember them.

"Let me." Fabiola reached past Devon to insert her passkey and tap the Level 1 on the panel. She leaned into his shoulder and nearly forced him off balance.

"You good with that, Devon?" Raphaël chuckled, and not in a friendly way. His voice was deep and his laughter deeper, filled with an ominous growl.

"What's with you, Raphaël? And you, Fabi? Be more careful." Devon readjusted his crutches for better balance.

"What's with you, Raphaël?" Mike "the hike" repeated. "Devon must not know they've cancelled the event this week, and that makes me wonder who got the Director riled up." He leaned in and sniffed of Devon's shoulder. "And is that *Annie* I smell on you? I didn't know Annie played so rough. But, like they say, break a leg. It's worth it every time."

Fabiola snickered.

Mike continued, "Do you need Fabi to help you off

the elevator, or can you manage that on your own?"

"His pet wolf will take care of him." Raphaël's deep voice ground the words in like sandpaper.

Garik drew in a sharp breath, and the changing colors in the elevator echoed his rising anger. He chanted to himself, *my anger, my control, I am better than that.*

"Keep calm. Don't do it."

Garik focused on Devon's subvocalized directive. He had known Garik would pick it up, but that no one else could.

"Don't do what?" Mike, with his big eyes, taunted Devon.

"Forgot he can hear super-low frequencies," Devon muttered.

"Pet wolf" hadn't bothered Garik as much as them making fun of Devon. What had the man done except help in any way he could, even spending an extended time in the hospital to cover for Garik's foul-up about the tablet? The colors in the elevator grew stronger, ever more vibrant, as Garik's anger shattered the light in the car into a rainbow cacophony. Before the number on the elevator door could fully light up to indicate their destination, Garik was in motion. The people around him froze as technicolor rainbows encased each person. Garik took Fabiola's hand and worked her fingers into Mike's hair. He felt in Raphaël's pocket for his pass-key, yanked Fabiola's from the control panel and inserted Raphaël's. He tucked the filched passkey into his pocket and pushed the icon for Basement Level 5, as far away from the Level 1 cafeteria as the elevator could take them with a hybrid's passkey. He was back at Devon's side before the Level 1 light reached full brightness, and he let the rainbows fade. The familiar exhaustion made him shaky, but the satisfaction from his revenge gave him a jolt of excitement.

The doors opened halfway, but before they completed their race to the sides, an alarm began to sound, and the doors stopped.

"Hey, woman." Mike. "Get your hand out of my hair!"

"Eu-wee, gross!" Fabiola gave a screech of disgust.

Garik glanced at Devon and grinned. He noted the red light blinking around the passkey, and a voice began, "Incorrect passkey. Please insert correct passkey now. Contacting security in five." A countdown began.

"Hey," Raphaël exclaimed. "Where's my passkey?"

"Let's go, Garik." Devon nodded.

Garik tried not to let them see his grin. He touched the doors, triggering them to fully retract, and he let Devon out ahead of him. Before he stepped away, he leaned over, pressed the close door icon, and released the doors before joining Devon.

"Hey, wait," Fabiola called as the door sealed her in.

"That was you, wasn't it?" Devon watched as the

indicator changed to Level 2, Level 3, Level 4, then Level 5. "They'll be right back, and we still have to eat breakfast with them."

"Maybe not that fast." Garik's synapses crackled with pleasurable energy. "Here's the passkey they need. I traded it for Raphaël's."

Devon began to smile. "I shouldn't find this funny. So, how fast *can* you move?"

"You saw. It does take it out of me." His head had begun to spin.

"No, I didn't see, only the results."

"I think I need food soon. You might want to get rid of the key."

He thought Devon took the passkey, but his power plant switched off about then, the lights went out, and he had no idea if Devon took it or not.

THANK GOODNESS for Ineke Van Steckelenburg. By the time Devon and Garik reached Level 1, Kevin Lee and several of the hybrids on his training schedule were gathered for breakfast. Ineke might seem aloof to those who didn't know her well, but she understood the importance of order, form, and presentation. Even from a distance, she saw Garik collapse at Devon's feet. That was out of order, and the crutches meant Devon was the plucky underdog in this story, the valiant underachiever who would try his best but never quite reach his goals.

Ineke commandeered Zekeria Salem, with his bowl-cut hair and youthful looks, to rescue the situation. Devon assured them he was certain the cure for what ailed the boy was food. He hadn't had breakfast, so?

By the time they had him at a table with food in front of him, Garik had his eyes open, and the story was unfolding. Lansana Opoku-Mensah, with her patterned scarification decorating her face, tilted her head and grumbled a personal embarrassment. "That man, sharing my elephant DNA and making me a humiliation unto myself."

"Is not your fault, girlfriend," Veronika Abbink consoled her. "You got the best of the genes, beauty and the ability to think. That man got his big nose from his elephant forebears, and he likes to trumpet his arrogance to everyone who will listen."

The round of laughter made things a little better, but Garik was uncomfortably aware of the mood across the cafeteria. Patches of hybrids congregated here and there, and storm clouds of frustration hovered darkly over them. They remained separated from the military personnel, scientists, and office workers, those people in the non-hybrid sector of the campus needed to keep the project running, even if they didn't have to endure the changes that kept their jobs secure.

Matches in a powder keg of tinder, ready to strike a flame and see how fast it burns.

Garik was reminded of the reason for the events on the mall and why the public never acquired tickets to attend. It was also the reason for the Tower's iconic lightshow, shattering the 40-story tower into a million shards of black glitter before reforming into the Tower to do it all over again. The human hybrids needed a place to let off steam, to be themselves, and to have no restrictions on being the person they had been modified to become. The events were wild because the hybrids were wilder. With the upcoming event cancelled, he hated to think where all these people would let out their steam. They would want someone to blame, and his picture was all over the protesters, literally. In every scene, they wore his face on their clothing, their placards, and likely their lips. If people wanted someone to blame, all fingers would point at him.

Garik didn't especially want to be himself right then, at least not in this place. And he was locked in, with hundreds of people who had little reason to like him.

Death at the hands of a fellow hybrid . . . not a fun way to go.

THE SPARKS Garik imagined speeding along the detonating cord were snuffed out by the appearance of Weston Rodheimer and Halo Sunchaser. The presence of the broad-shouldered Director and his tall, hawk-like second-in-command had a way of smothering every other activity. Rodheimer's face darkened at the sight of Garik beside Devon, although he didn't call him out.

"We need muscle to complete the clean up to the parking garage. Melanie, Chris." He pointed to two people, who stood. He looked across the breakfast crowd, called out, "Joachim, you, Lansana, Ineke and Stephen. Come with me. Where are Raphaël and Mike?"

Raphaël, Fabiola, and Mike appeared, escorted by a security guard.

"What's happened here?" Sunchaser. "Security? Why is that necessary?"

From a distance, another security guard near the elevator held up something too small to see, unless you had a hawk's telescopic vision, and yelled, "Found it!"

"Oh," Sunchaser said with thinly veiled bitterness. "A passkey. I wonder how that got lost."

Garik looked up to see her eyes boring into him. He wanted to melt into his seat. Her intent was clear. He had been with Marisa when she had "borrowed" Sunchaser's key the first time they visited the Tower. Using it was what had gotten him inducted into the human-hybrid program—and, he suspected, earned Sunchaser a reprimand for losing a highly sensitive and important piece of electronic wizardry.

When Rodheimer and Sunchaser left with their team of workers, Devon leaned in, "I'm glad I disposed of that key. I'd hate for them to have found it on you."

His words didn't make Garik feel much better. When Devon had messed up and wrecked his car, he'd wound up in the hospital and now wore a full leg cast. If Garik messed up, he might well find himself facing Halo Sunchaser's electrified sword. He pictured Rodheimer—the Silverback!—with his fingers discharging bolts of electricity into the sword, charging it up, and the sword flashing out and dissolving someone atom by atom until they were nothing.

It had happened. Garik had been forced to watch. He didn't want it to be him next.

Houdini time, anyone? He needed to get out of this place, if only he could figure a way. The Tower's exits were locked tight, but surely there was a crack in the façade somewhere.

The laughter resumed around him, but the darkness in Garik's head was hard to drive away.

— 4 —

vents under Corona Tower continued their downhill
slide. As it went across Bay City aboveground, so the
dusty depths followed.

Of course, no bombs exploded in the underground
research center. Nor did open fights or demonstrations
erupt among the human-hybrid participants in the program.

The tension, however, was something you could
feel. The awareness of who walked the corridors with

you; the group members sitting at the next table; locking your door to your quarters where at other times it wouldn't have occurred to you.

Devon was going nuts in the apartment, and Garik convinced him to try a Segway, determined to stay out and about with the people he had befriended.

"Look, Dev-o, it's easy-o." Garik stepped up on the personal transport device and back off. It remained perfectly still and level the entire time, not tilting once.

"Easy for you to say. I'm guessing I've been driving you bonkers with the kiddo stuff, huh?" Devon held one side of the handle, giving the computerized machine a doubtful glare.

"Why?" The unit didn't have a custom wall charger. It had to be plugged in each night, and Garik dropped to his back to work the cord between a chair and a small table. The wall next to his ZBoard charging station didn't quite hold the larger Segway, and Devon had refused to consider parking it in his bedroom.

"Oh, Dev-o. Easy-o. That type of stuff." Devon drew in a deep breath and released it, a tired sound.

"Hey, no." Garik plugged the unit into the wall and jumped to his feet. He brushed his hands off and then the sleeve of his shirt. He smiled at the morose expression devouring Devon's face. "You're my friend-o, Dev-o," and he clapped him on the upper arm, then balled his hand and punched his shoulder.

"That's kind, but it's not fair to you. I'm in a position of power as your activity director, and that makes us not even. You have to be friends with me."

"That's a good one. Make me laugh at something else. Now get on the Segway."

"Seriously. You don't have to be friends with me. I know how this works."

"What's with you? You're not activity anything right now. Broken leg, remember? Full cast? Kevin Lee? He took your job, at least until you get better, and with you refusing to get on this freedom machine, that might be forever. I'm friends with you because I want to try to save your sorry attitude from getting me equally depressed. Let's go do something, the pool, watch people train, cheer them on. Quit moping, and let's get out of this hamster cage."

"Hamster cage." Devon looked around. "Didn't know I lived in a hamster cage. You could go with Kevin. He could use your help."

"Kevin has enough enthusiasm for two people. You sit on the couch all day, and when I go with Kevin, I find you in the exact same spot when I get back. Do you even get up at all?"

"Um, yeah. The bathroom is in there." He pointed through his bedroom.

"And then you come right back to the couch."

"Okay, yeah." Devon shrugged.

"I'm saving you from that, friend-o. Now get on-o."

Devon took a deep breath and decided his good leg

needed to go on first, but he leaned too hard into the steering arm and it twisted, toppled forward, and he tumbled straight down.

"I told you!" Devon balled a hand and smashed the floor.

"And I told you. It's easy-o." Garik reached for his hand to help him to his feet to start over.

"And enough with the 'o' after all your words. I get it."

"Right-o, Devon-o." Garik continued to hold out his hand.

"Sheesh. Why I ever agreed for you to share my apartment—"

"I got you doing it!" Garik hooted. Devon frowned as Garik grasped his hand and pulled him to his feet, light as a feather. "You're using my words. Excellent!"

"God help me, I'm becoming you."

"Only if you can bark." Garik caught his eye and grinned. "See, I can find it funny, too. I don't like being here, but it's not all bad. I miss my friends outside, and I wish I hadn't been recaptured, but every now and then, I like a little bit of it."

"That day we first met, remember?" Devon's eyes had gone shiny.

"The climbing wall? How could I forget? I was mortified."

"Remember what I told you?"

"That I couldn't climb? No, I remember. You said

even Amy could climb the red route."

"Sorry for that. No, I said I might even like you if you stuck around." He shrugged. "Well, you stuck around."

"And?" Garik teased as Devon focused on the personal mobility device.

"And what?" He rocked the steering arm, letting it resettle each time, and taking a deep breath.

"Do you like me now?"

"I'm not on this mobile death trap, yet. We'll see." But he grinned.

"I should push you over just to see you fall. Here, bootie on first, then your real foot. I'll hold it till you balance. There, got it?"

Devon looked dubious but he was standing and balanced on the Segway. He said, "Now what?"

"We go and say hi to the world." Garik took his ZBoard from its station, dropped it to the floor, and hopped on. He motioned for Devon to follow, and they headed out the door.

THEY STAYED in Corona City to start. Devon was familiar with the area, and there wouldn't be any surprises, especially with most people at their places of employment or training on one of the lower floors.

Several times, Garik had to encourage the older man. "Lean into it to go faster." Or, "It's just a curb, Devon. It'll go right over. Trust your machine."

Garik convinced him to practice in both of Corona City's parks. Across grass, up and over walkways, and in one place, over a curved footbridge that crossed an artificial stream. On the way down, the Segway built some speed, and Garik called, "Just lean back."

The second park held the Corona City pool surrounded with plantings and small trees. "I've not been here before. Very pretty," he called to Devon, and he stepped off his skateboard to explore. A skylight the size of the pool jutted two stories upwards. He remembered this from the outside, a big service block of a structure. Before living underground, Garik had never dreamed it topped an indoor pool in an underground park.

"Okay, I'm still over here. Broken leg. Yoo-hoo."

"Segway." Garik motioned with his hand.

"Curb."

"Lean into it." Garik pantomimed. "I'll rescue you if you fall."

"I'll expect you to follow through."

When Garik heard the wheels crunch beside him, he pointed up. "That should be clear, right?" He had expected to see blue, and the sky through the glass roiled with gray.

"Should be." Devon followed his hand, and the Segway began rolling backwards.

Garik took the handle and steadied it. "Smoke, maybe?" With what was happening in the city, that worried him.

"Burning leaves, perhaps. People do rake and burn them." A crashing sound beyond the glass two stories overhead said otherwise.

"Not leaves. Be quiet for a moment." Garik listened to see if he could pick up on anything to help determine the cause.

"A car crash?" Devon smiled helpfully.

Black smoke began to billow over half of the glassed expanse. "I didn't hear any breaking glass, and the smoke wouldn't look like that."

"That makes sense."

"Where's the nearest Internet access?" Garik berated himself. The blank corridors and basement "streets," mostly empty. He had been so focused on Devon's riding skills that he had eclipsed everything else from his awareness. Now, somehow, they had missed out on something vital happening outside. With everything else that had taken place, there was no way it didn't involve him, and the only way outside was through Devon's non-hybrid Net access.

"My place. Or anywhere with a hardwired computer. I would need to log in."

"What's closest? The gaming center?" Garik had begun to run toward his ZBoard, calling, "Keep up if you can."

He tried not to outpace the half-crippled man too badly, but Garik wasn't so far gone from Russia that he didn't remember what burning buildings sounded like, and Kevin had kept them abreast of the increasing tension throughout Bay City. He felt it in the marrow of his bones.

They were barely started when Kevin appeared. He was in his soccer clothes, a white tee, black shorts, and tall white socks, with athletic shoes. Paul Gberie matched him, and as he ran, he kept morphing his skin color and texture to the surrounding walls, a clear sign of his urgency. The third person Kevin breathlessly introduced as Joachim Warakaulle, a man with a South Pacific vibe, with skin color and hair to match. Kevin took time to explain that he and Paul had been putting in extra time in a soundproof training cell, and Joachim had been sent to find them to get them to the lobby. Everyone was there. That's when Kevin knew he had to search for Garik and Devon, and *what are you guys doing way out here, anyway? Didn't you notice everyone gone?*

"Practice," Garik answered, "on the Segway," as they headed toward the elevator.

NOT EVERYONE was upstairs, but Garik understood what Kevin meant. All the human hybrids and many of their instructors, aides, and medical facilitators, anyone, basically, not from Level 5, the hospital, or the research labs. Even a scattering of military types and clerical office personnel were present.

Televisions had been rolled out, with large screens, revealing just why so few uniforms were on the floor with them. The different screens showed various snapshots of Bay City, but they all revealed the same story. People were running, some holding placards aloft, and others attempting to get out of the way. A number carried flaming Molotov cocktails, and occasionally someone would throw one, and it would smash through a storefront. Firetrucks pumped water on burning buildings, but there were so many aflame that how could they put them all out?

It was impossible to make out individual people. Some of the buildings, yes. The Luncheon Lady, aflame. The City Transportation Depot was blackened on one side, as if a fire had started but hadn't taken hold before being extinguished. One of the big old houses on Pill Hill, the roof crashed in. A tornado of sparks spun skyward. It would soon be consumed by the flames.

What had Garik heard burning near the pool's skylight in Corona City? It was mostly residential, except for the area to the north where the supposed back entrance to the underground research center was located. Even that wasn't likely noticeable from the pool, as it would be blocks away.

Then there it was, a giant effigy of the Tower, right there in the middle of Stamford, beams and logs and crates piled into a towering bonfire, blazing away.

"Look at that," Garik whispered. "Someone wanted

to send someone a warning."

"*We* burned it." The rumble of Rodheimer's voice broke Garik's focus on the television screen.

"Why? The rioters are the ones causing the damage. Why would you make it worse?"

"Look again, my boy. A rescue attempt, I believe. A scaffolding, perhaps for a crane. Tell me, boy, who would they wish to rescue?"

"I don't know." Garik was truly frightened.

"The deeper we go, the more difficult I find it to believe a word you say."

When Garik unearthed the courage to look around, the Director was gone. The carnage on the screens still ruled. Bay City was coming apart. Who knew when it would end?

— 5 —

he talk rose and fell as people pointed to new atrocities, letting themselves be pulled from screen to screen like puppets on a string. Eventually, the shock faded, and a few people wandered off to sit in the cafeteria—set off from the main lobby by a large, arched doorway some hundred feet wide and nearly to the ceiling—or make their way to an elevator or drop to the floor in groups of two or three.

Garik, Devon, Kevin, and Joachim wandered into

the cafeteria where the blare of the rioting in the city was muted. The televisions continued to shift from atrocity to atrocity, revealing the slashing destruction being torn into Bay City's skin like a samurai's sword cutting to the bone, but it was easier to not look.

Garik found it harder not to listen, and the yelling and sounds of destruction were a mallet banging his skull. He found it easier to stare into space, his eyes seeing the tables, the serving lines, the cleanup areas, and the kitchens that opened to the rest of the room.

The only way to truly avoid the screens was to keep them to his back. Joachim sat in a chair across from Garik, studying him, while the two "normals" discussed life outside the basement complex, with Devon pressing Kevin for what he knew.

"What?" Garik grew irritated at Joachim's attention.

"Nothing." The man grinned and looked away.

"No, what? You're not looking at me like that for nothing."

"I'm not looking at you, man. Out there, that's where I'm looking." He tilted his head toward the screens in the lobby.

"Not a minute ago, you weren't." Garik had first seen the man with his skin and hair and felt a kinship. Different ethnicity but different in the same way Garik's bronze skin and curly mop of hair made him, ostracized by people who didn't like things that were "different" to intrude on their safe little lives.

"You sitting so wrapped up in all this." Joachim waved his hand around him, indicating the two activity directors and the screens blaring the news from the outside.

"I am wrapped up in all this." Garik narrowed his eyes, his anger overcoming his dismay at the images he'd seen of Bay City's undoing. "Did you pay attention to any of that? Those people are protesting because of me. That's my name on those placards, my picture on their shirts and signs."

"Yeah, man, I noticed." Joachim leaned forward, and he looked side to side as if checking for people who might overhear. "I've seen all this before. The overlords." His eyes moved to take in what he could see of the upper floor of the basement that stretched around them for acres and acres. "Us, the peons, here just because they say we can be here. Then, there's those guys—" he pointed to where the screens still let the outside leak in, "—who think they can right every wrong and save us. They don't even think that maybe we don't want to be saved. What do you think about that?"

"Sounds like nonsense to me. I want to be saved."

"That right, huh, man?" Joachim leaned back, and he stretched one arm over the back of an adjacent chair. "Then why aren't you out there cheering them on? I don't see that from anybody here. Nope." He swiveled his head and looked around. He leaned in again. "And you know why? All those people don't want to rescue you. Nope, not in a heartbeat."

"But—" Garik tried to work out the man's logic. They were torching the city in his name. "Of course—"

"I see you're working on it up there. It just hasn't become pudding yet." Joachim reached and tapped Garik's forehead with his knuckles. "Now, let me tell you how this goes. One, those people out there get what they want. This place turns throat up, gives in, and *they* get to walk in and take what they want. You, me, even, and maybe a lot of people in here. Not all, mind you, because some of us come from far away just to get done to us what was done to you. Maybe we don't want rescued, and maybe they don't want to rescue us, but supposing they do. What do they get, tell me that, man?"

"I get to go home." Just talking about it made Garik want it more than ever.

"But do you? That's the hundred-dollar question. I was there when Rodheimer gave you that pat on the back."

Pat on the back. Garik forced his gears to shift. What pat on the back?

"Not as bright as we thought, is he?" Joachim grinned, asking no one and, in the same breath, asking everyone.

"What pat?"

"Your welcome home. 'One of our own has

returned to us,' that type of welcome."

"That." He remembered the first night after his recapture. All the hybrids had been required to gather in the lobby. That was the night when Sunchaser and her electrified sword had sucked up a condemned hybrid and melted her into the nothingness of atomic dissolution. "I'm on the outs with him now."

"Sure, you would be, all that nonsense outside. Tell me, when you were out, did you get the welcome you wanted?"

Seeing Marisa in the shop washed over him, and he studied the floor. His dismay at her rejection, the chase, and his recapture.

"Don't answer. I can see it. Man, you've got to know that they don't want you. They want what you used to be, and you can never be that again. This place gave you a new life, well, for you, maybe stole your old one to do it, but that doesn't change that you can't go back. You're one of us now, man."

"What's way number two?"

"Okay, you're sharper than I give you credit. Power doesn't give up power without a fight. Way number two is Rodheimer or whoever is in control—"

"Whoever?" Garik jerked his head up. "He's the Director."

"Yah, man, but he don't fund the place. Get what I mean? *Whoever* is in control opens the taps, and out flood the guns, the troops, whatever they need to get back control. That's way number two. Don't think they won't do it."

"They're already out there. Those people are military, Air Force, likely, even in those black suits—" Garik cut off his tirade. He didn't *know*, but it made sense. Who else could they send out?

"There's always more." Joachim nodded his head several times.

"You guys?" Garik crossed his arms on the table and rested his chin on them. He glanced at several groups doing the same as they were, trying to work though the events pounding at Bay City's infrastructure.

"Ha! That's wishful thinking." Joachim seemed to find Garik's suggestion a good joke.

"Isn't that what this is for, training people for military exercises?"

"Hey, man, everyone knows the people you left out there. Hefferly can pretend to fit in, but you think that Justin dude can even be around people without them wanting to know what Rodheimer is doing to people down here? Even down here. You can pass, and maybe me, but Mike with those eyes? Jacquelien? No, no, maybe Paul. Get Paul up there, and no one's going to look at him twice, is that it? We're not superheroes. We're freaks, at least to them. That's why the events, so we can pretend to dress up, but really it's just us, normal in one way, but bizarre freaks of nature to anyone on the outside."

Garik kept his eyes on Devon for a moment, still tight in conversation with Kevin, attempting to get his head around the man considering him a freak of nature. Then, Kevin. If Garik grew a tail and howled at the moon, would he still claim him as a friend? Marisa didn't even know, and she'd dropped him right into the Tower's clutches. With her arm twisted, he was convinced, but still. Here he was back in the Tower's grasp.

"Then why bring everyone up here if they aren't going to be part of the plan? I don't get that. If they're planning to keep us sealed in here like microbes in a laboratory, why bother? Let us train, and that's the end of it. We don't know, and we're better off for it."

"Support, I think, and mental conditioning. The idea that if anyone gets a notion that out there's better, that's what the reality is. We're better off here." He shrugged. "Maybe. It looks the way you want depending on where you're standing."

Noise in the main lobby caught their attention, and they saw several black-suited men show up and begin rolling the televisions to the side. They were still broadcasting the events on ground level, so they weren't being disconnected, more as if they were in the way.

"What now?" Paul appeared at a neighboring table, literally appeared, as if shifting from one light spectrum to another.

"Oh, it's you." Joachim looked annoyed. "Rude

boy, that's you, man. You hiding in plain sight? Not cool."

Paul was once again in his beaded tunic. It shifted from imitating a table and chair a fraction of a second after Paul appeared. He laughed, causing Devon and Kevin to look his direction.

"I must practice my skills. I am getting better. What is happening?" He pointed to the commotion in the lobby.

"I'm guessing you overheard. Do you need me to repeat it?" Joachim drummed his fingers on the table.

"Predict, not restate." Paul smiled, revealing the gold letters inset into his front teeth. He winked at Garik and called to Kevin. "As a *teammate*, may I inquire what my *teammate* predicts is about to happen?"

"No idea." Kevin shrugged. He stood and joined the dozen others from across the room who were headed to the door for a closer look. "Bet it's good. Come see."

"I will wait for you to discover and share." He shifted his attention to Garik and Joachim. "I have a joke I wish to share with you. You will find this very funny. Two chickens come upon an egg in the middle of the road—"

Before he could go further, booted feet began to echo in the hard-walled space. The sleek furniture, bright colors, and modern art that gave the area a museum-like hush receded with the press of black-suited men in full riot control gear. The entire area darkened, although the lights didn't change brightness. Each one wore a face shield with three metal bands across the smoked surface, a black helmet, and an active response shooter vest over a multi-threat body armor vest. A tactical backpack with entry tools dotted the shoulders of a quarter of the men, and many wore Damascus-style hard shell armor, including knee and shin guards, or carried some portion of it in one hand. Among them were various weapons, including pneumatic blaster guns and several spooling guns. Two men shouldered detonation cannons, normally used to dispel flocks of birds, but the prospects were endless when the flocks were of the human type.

A tall man, bulkier with muscle than his companions, took a position at the front. "Ready?" he called.

"Ready, sir," the team replied as one.

The leader turned, and they began to run in step towards the military housing section of the Level 1 portion of the basement, only to turn at the last minute and disappear into the corridor leading to the underground parking garage where the military-style and tactical vehicles were parked.

Garik had two thoughts when he saw the last man vanish into the distance. One, that was a lot of force for a security team already dispersed throughout Bay City. Where had they come from? With their helmets and gear, it was impossible to identify them.

Two, access from the parking garage to the military quarters was direct and did not route through the lobby. The chances of the men being military were unlikely.

Three, he remembered Devon's observation. Most of the tactical vehicles in the garage couldn't navigate the parking garage egress up and through the above-ground parking garage. These men were taking a different way out.

He wanted to follow, to be with them, to Houdini out the parking garage using the secret exit. But that was possible only if he had a riot-control suit to wear.

And just like everything else down here, he had no idea where he would find one of those.

Life as Garik, a looming disaster in every way.

— 6 —

everal of the screens could be seen from inside the cafeteria, revealing reporters talking to viewers, their neatly coiffed hair belying the grime and blackened disease of disruption invading the city behind them.

Garik's attention was drawn to a drone shot of the mayhem. The camera hovered over the city, focused on Central Park and the garbage and broken tents left by the protesters. Fires had stained the playground equipment with blackened soot, in several places still trailing smoke into the air; and plastic bags, one in purple clearly stamped Fasst Market, floated at the edge of the duck pond. A lone duck prodded it, perhaps hoping for a tasty snack.

The image shifted—a different drone, likely—to the blocked-off area between First and Ninth, the "Take the City" Tower Free Zone. The camera panned south, and Garik could just see the roof of City View Apartments. His heart skipped a beat, and his back tingled. He imagined he might find Marisa on the roof looking out over the disruption, perhaps even observing the very drone looking back at her, a link of a sort between him and her. A connection. A renewal of what once was, not Joachim's acerbic accusation that she would have no interest in him as he was, only in what he had been.

He saw the truth in it, however. There was no Marisa on the roof of City View Apartments. From City View's vantage point, most of Bay City was hidden. Taller structures dominated the apartment building, blocking the light, the air, the life from it. Garik quickly pushed his last encounter with Marisa to the deepest part of his mind, shut it away as if it had never happened. It was a betrayal of them, of their time together, of the dreams he had once had—still had!—of their possible future together.

Then the camera rocked downward as the drone began a flyover of the barricaded area. Flattop buildings were drizzled with ocher and gray, weather-stained; and in the shadows of roof parapets and air conditioning units, remnants of snow hunkered for safety against the sun. Bare tree branches cast spidery shadows on concrete sidewalks. Open-top barrels stood in the center of several streets. One was ablaze as people huddled around, warming themselves with gloves, mufflers, and toboggans. They seemed oblivious to what was happening elsewhere in the city.

Crossing Ninth to the north, the luxurious cul-de-sacs of Shady Ridge Acres were business as usual, the tennis courts and swimming pools, several covered, and as many open and glittering with reflected sky. The divide between rich and poor. The haves and have-nots. The peons and the overlords . . . the power brokers, the Weston Rodheimers of the city.

The view slipped down the hillside past West Corona, over Starnes and Richardson and the parking lots at Waldorf's Department Store, filled as if protests weren't happening elsewhere in the city. Richies unite! Let nothing get in the way of shopping for more luxury goods to pack our over-filled homes!

Then Waldorf's was gone, and Garik tried to imagine where the drone was headed. The riot control troops that had just left the Tower . . . the drone traveling north . . . the only thing that direction was the waterfront. The Docks. Harbor Shipyards. Then there was Argyle Station to the west, with Interstate Transport nearby. Both were vital to The Docks and the Shipyards, and

The Docks and the Shipyards to them. They were the life of Bay City, its reason to exist, or at least the reason a hundred years ago. Now the city had Corona Tower, Bay City Medical, Ransom Communications, Ai Kee! and a hundred other businesses, but the waterfront remained essential to all the rest.

The drone's camera fell into the sweeping bend of Shorefront Boulevard on its way to the four massive piers of The Docks, crowded with overhead cranes and warehouses. Garik knew the area, one of the places he and Maria had liked to explore. Why show this to the world if things were normal, under control and operational?

Soon, the monitor revealed a warehouse in flames and a tractor-trailer rig twisted awkwardly, spilling boxes of electronic goods. People were looting, even as the drone's camera panned them, zooming in to reveal two men wedging a large, flat television box into the back of an open-top Jeep. Without strapping it down, they jumped inside and sped away. One of the men held the box against the wind.

Along the bottom of the screen, a banner scrolled: "Hundreds descend on The Docks, disrupting commerce in and out of the city. Harbor Shipyards closed after bomb threat. Interstate Transport officials say the economic impact could soon be felt across the western half of the United States."

"Still want to be out there?"

Like waking from a nightmare, the question jerked Garik's attention back into the pandemonium of the lobby. Paul Gberie was beside him; and more people, most he was unfamiliar with, watched the video feed with them.

"It's bad." It was worse than bad, but his comprehension was eclipsed. He never expected Bay City—his home!—to ever experience what he had run from in his Russian homeland.

"Did you miss the shock troops?" Paul cocked an eye Garik's direction. "Bet they show up on those cameras if we wait on them."

"The ones headed to the—" He almost said secret exit, and he clamped his words off. "The ones we just saw?"

"Getting smarter by the minute." Paul laughed, and he gave Garik's shoulder a good slap, causing him to nearly stumble. "Come. Some friends and I have a theory. Since you're key—by your own description—we want you part of our discussion."

As Garik turned to follow Paul, the scene on the screen zoomed out, and black suits began to tumble from military-type transports. They spread out in hopes of containing the virus invading the waterfront.

Garik was no longer certain it could be done.

"YOU KNOW Jacquelien and Bert," Paul threw out casually before they reached the group sitting around one of the clean and modern "conversation" groupings in the bright, museum-like lobby.

"Like I could forget." He pictured them, Jacqueline with a red line tattooed down her face and Bert with hair even a punk rocker would enjoy rocking.

"And the reason they aren't with the shock troops fighting the war." Paul pricked Garik with his reminder.

Garik felt the prick and accepted it as justified. Still, war. The implication was ominous. As they approached their destination, Garik was distracted by six striking hybrids he had never met, all no less forgettable than the two he already knew.

He had begun to realize that the friends he'd helped escape the Tower were normal by comparison, well, with the possibility of Justin, and Justin with his praying mantis wings was outrageous by even a hybrid's broad measure.

"What's your beauty mark, sweetie?"

Garik located the speaker, a woman with emerald hair and bright, iridescent patches over her skin. She studied him through emerald-green eyes. Body suit? He suspected that down here, no one would bother, not unless they were attending an event, and this weekend's had been cancelled.

"Forgive Charlotte." Paul apologized for the woman, but his skin morphed into an angry, mottled red. He called to her, "Chill, pill. You're not a beauty, yourself."

"Yah, just ribbing. You're okay, sweetie. Come meet the bunch of us. We're nicer than that loser you're with."

Two lookalikes, tall, dark-haired brothers, with pale skin and full features, likely twins, smiled at the tease. One, with a hair-free break in his right eyebrow, touched his brother. The other, with a small mole by his left eye, seemed more reserved. He nodded and removed his brother's hand from his arm.

"Anatoli and Andrey, meet Garik. Garik, the twins."

"*Garik, the twins.*" Anatoli with the eyebrow repeated Paul's words, an exact mimicry.

"And we are *Anatoli and Andrey.*" Andrey mirrored his brother when he recited their names, and he also could have been Paul speaking.

"That's good." Garik laughed. "Parrots?"

"They. Can. Parrot." A pretty woman with coffee skin, a dark halo of hair, and long legs looked down at them. They were tall. She was taller. She clipped her words as if each was a sentence all on its own. "Melanie. Hatherill. If. Paul. Doesn't. See. Fit. To. Tell. You."

"Garik, meet Melanie Hatherill. She runs really well." Paul's skin now rippled blue with laughter.

"I've. Heard. You. Are. Faster."

"Maybe. Glad to meet you, Melanie." Then and there, Garik decided. These people had a status quo among them, a pecking order, and he didn't plan to be at the bottom of it. He would be if he didn't assert himself. He put a little attitude into his bark, calling, "Anatoli and Andrey," to get their attention.

"*Anatoli and Andrey*." Anatoli could have been Garik speaking.

"Funny how you can do that, but I didn't get your last names. Do you have one?"

"Anati?" Andrey nudged his brother. "Do we?"

"If you can pronounce it, *sweetie*," he barbed.

When the man said sweetie, Garik heard the shift in his voice. He mimicked Charlotte. The woman frowned.

"My last name is Shayk. I'm pretty sure I can handle whatever you throw at me. Shoot, I'm listening." Van Hermoso, his occupational therapist, had used that phrase.

"Bur-gor-ski—" Anatoli drew it out like he was sure Garik couldn't handle it, or he wanted to mock him. Garik wasn't sure, and he cut him off.

"Burgorski. My mother's sister's married name. Simple. For the rest of you, if you want to meet me, last name, please. I've got a good memory and I won't forget." At the same time, he etched the Burgorski twins in his mind, picturing his grandmother's twin dolls Annie and Andy skiing down a booger of a mountain. He was certain he would remember.

Charlotte raised a chartreuse finger, and she offered, "Mnich," with a grin.

"Got it, Charlotte Mnich." Garik said three times to himself, Charlotte Mean Witch. He grinned at the image.

Louise King wore flowing robes, likely a coverup, Garik decided, though for what he couldn't imagine. Her face's patterned colors gave her a royal presence, and he pictured her on a throne. Louise King was stamped in his memory.

The final hybrid was Chris Beer, a man whose long, coarse hair and thick-soled boots gave him a workman's stance. He prefaced his introduction with, "Oh-h-h-h," almost like a horse's neigh, and then gave his name. Garik pictured the man at an old-fashioned western bar ordering a beer, meaning the man would forever be Chris Beer in Garik's mind.

THE GROUP'S theory didn't fall too far from Garik's own. He didn't reveal Kevin's part in jumpstarting the protesters, but they knew Jantzen Hefferly, the one-time second-in-command of the human-hybrid research complex, was on the outside. The man had a reputation as a Loki-type prankster, someone who liked to prod the system to get the results he wanted.

They also asked about Joanie McDonald, with her mohawk and swaggering half-phrases. Likely, she would do all this, right? And Alyna Lindberg, with her vicious Komodo dragon claws . . . they described damage they had seen that could only be Alyna.

Each of Garik's fellow escapees got thrown into the discussion's volatile blender. Julia Cantos, Giselle Harmon, Amy Howe and more.

Louise was especially interested in John Carter, a larger-than-life blond god, even fitter than Devon Maye had been before his confinement in his one-legged cast. Garik heard her emotions when she spoke his name, literally heard them. Her heart pounded faster, her pores opened to expel excess warmth, and she gave off the faintest papery rustle when she put her hands to her face to pat her flushed cheeks.

Garik hadn't imagined John with an admirer. He wondered if the man knew. He grinned. It would be a good thing to store away. He could tease him when they next met.

And they would soon, he was certain of that.

— 7 —

he nightmare taking over Bay City didn't remain in Bay City.

A security team all in black entered the austere and modern lobby with its displays of cutting-edge sculptures and widely spaced seating areas. Closer to the cafeteria entrance, the television displays still hawked the outside disruptions, hoping to sell the horror to anyone they could draw in, but nearer Garik and his new acquaintances, quiet and organization ruled. That made the four black goons stand out like black beans in a sea of white. Weapons dangling from their belts shifted with an ominous sound, suggesting heavily armored protection they couldn't see.

The four goons drew up sharply, and Garik could hear their joints lock into place, prepared for resistance, and determined not to let it deter them from their mission.

The lead goon spoke.

"Major Judy Kennedy. And this is Captain Ryan Lee." The captain didn't nod or give any indication he had been introduced. His shirt said Lee, the only way to tell which of the three people accompanying the major was the captain, unless they wanted to look for rank insignia. She didn't see fit to introduce the final two, so likely they were far down the totem pole. "Garik Shayk, will you please stand? Director Rodheimer requires your attendance."

"For?" Garik wasn't military, and he understood the Director held all the power, but he wasn't sure it was military power.

"Not mine to say. If you will." She took one step back, as if allowing Garik the room to join her.

Garik looked at the people around him, inquiring with his eyes if they had anything to offer to explain this. In the distance, the cafeteria held its arms around Devon and Kevin, the two people he knew and trusted best. They were too far to offer him any help.

"Paul?" Garik stood, and he turned his full attention to the colorful man. He noted his adaptation enabling him to blend into any background scenario was now tuned to mimic the security team. It wasn't exact but not far off, either. Garik understood the pointed joke, the mimicry that made fun of the people who dared to step into the hybrid's world to make them dance to a tune they didn't hear or care about.

"Ship to, my young'un," Paul said with a mocking tone, as his face shifted into a bearded pirate. "Else they'll have you walking the plank soon's the sharks snap their shiny teeth." He laughed, bowed as if accepting adulations for a stage performance, and offered his hand. "Watch for that sword," he whispered, and he winked. "I hear it has quite a kick."

"Thanks." Garik wanted to roll his eyes, and he fought the impulse. Then he turned to face Kennedy. "Ma'am."

It seemed ominous, a black cloud, when Kennedy and Lee took his left and right flank, and the other two fell in behind. The feeling was old coffee, staining the moment, hard to swallow. Like he might try to get away, perhaps run for the hills, make this his opportunity to Houdini once again and be gone from here.

He would if the opportunity presented itself. He let his eyes scan the area as they walked, hoping, yet nothing appeared to him. He was a blind person being led into the darkness. Even his quickness was no good to him when he had nowhere to run.

He couldn't get one thing out of his thoughts. What could the military want with him? The last time he had seen Colonel Brace and the Director in the same room, they had been at one another's throats.

Blackened grounds of dread swirled at the bottom of Garik's cup, and he expected it to be bitter when he was finally forced to drink it down.

"ABOUT TIME." Rodheimer's growled greeting grated across the room.

"Sir." Major Kennedy nodded, and she turned to Colonel Brace, also in the room. "Colonel, is that all?"

"Thank you, Major. Please wait outside with your team. I may need your services again."

"Yessir." She saluted and backed out of the room, leaving Garik with the two men. The tension was a brewing thunderstorm, and electricity crackled in the air. Brace broke the tightly tuned silence first.

"Mr. Shayk, tell me your predictions. Why are you here?" His tone said this was a test.

"Um, your person out there said to come?" Garik had been cowed when walking with the four goons, but Brace was sandpaper on his nerves. He felt his attitude growing spikes, and he wasn't sure he cared. What good had these two ever done him? And what could they do *to* him? Besides the electrified sword, and if they wanted that, he suspected Sunchaser would be here, also.

"Understand, Mr. Shayk," Brace said, his feathers clearly ruffled, "you have been a promise unfulfilled since your arrival. I have been convinced not to terminate your line of research only because I have been assured your development would indeed be worth the investment. Convince me."

Garik looked to Rodheimer, saw a dark cloud hanging over him, and knew he would have no help there. Something had happened between the two men before he arrived, and Garik was to be the tiebreaker. Or they would break him, whichever made them happy. He suspected Brace would rather break him, even if it meant losing whatever unfinished battle was taking place between them.

He recalled an earlier conversation between the two men. Rodheimer had insisted the situation in Bay City was under control, and Brace had mocked his assurances. They had only ended the escalating confrontation when the Tower had come under attack and the parking garage on Stamford Drive had gone down in a haze of broken bricks and powdered concrete, the victim of a protestor's well-placed bomb.

The situation between the two men took on a clarity that Garik should have seen then. Rodheimer was fighting for control of the project, and Brace was determined to wrest it from him. Opportunity was his only roadblock, and the events in the city were eroding that roadblock as surely as a torrent of water rushing from behind a shattered dam.

Garik had to tread carefully. He was on the knife edge, with Rodheimer on the left and Brace on the right. To slip down the wrong way was to cut himself to the bone. These men wouldn't care, not about him.

He decided not to hold back.

"So, Colonel Brace, about your backup plans to take over once the protesters do enough damage—" That was all he needed to say to crack the man's stone face, and Brace exploded.

"How dare you, Director! Our dealings are a matter of the utmost confidentiality. You would ply this boy against me, use one of your *experiments* to embarrass me?" Brace's composure had broken, and his cheeks turned red.

"You are a fool, Brace." Rodheimer's shoulders seemed to broaden, as if his muscles were tightening for a fight. He crackled with electricity. "What could I have said to him? Your people retrieved him. It seems you required prescience of him. Perhaps his foresight told him what you've attempted to hide from me."

"It is impossible. The boy is guessing."

"As Christian did?"

Garik's attention lit up at the mention of the man's name. Christian had also been melded with canine DNA, although from a wolfhound rather than a timber wolf. He had developed precognition skills—prescience—and been deemed a failure. Christian had no drive to use his far-seeing skills to further military intervention in world affairs, and he had been shipped off to *somewhere* to be further used in research.

"Christian was a false hope." Brace had regained much of his composure. "This one, I fear, is no better."

The man had been assured Garik's development would provide what the military needed, a successful precog with the tractability to be amenable to the military's rigorous demands. Or, in other words, to do the dirty work of guiding the killers that would keep Brace and his cohorts firmly embedded in the halls of military power.

"He knows about your backup plan."

It was interesting to Garik that the Director didn't seem especially concerned about whatever Brace was planning. Perhaps the Director had an ace up his sleeve, his own backup plan, on the off chance that the military did step into the quagmire of conquest over the human-hybrid program.

"There is no backup plan." Brace's face was expressionless. "I want what is best for the Air Force's investment, and not only the Air Force, but every division of the nation's military forces."

Garik heard the lie, in the man's breathing, his heartbeat, and the way he exhaled a sharp breath at the end of each sentence. He was, however, out of his familiar territory, and he didn't know how to step on only the stones that would keep him from falling into the quicksand. He also wasn't convinced Rodheimer was the good guy in this situation, so why should he help him?

Rodheimer made his choice for him with his next sentence.

"The boy is the cause of all this." Rodheimer pressed something on his desk, and one wall exploded into a giant image of the events outside the basement research center. He touched the desk again, and different parts of the image zoomed in, revealing Garik's name and image blasted across the scenes of protest. "Somehow, he has fostered people's natural sympathies, and this is the result. I had hoped his alleged deportation to Russia would eliminate any possibility of this, but then Jantzen aided the boy in escape, and my carefully orchestrated plan evaporated. This boy is the one to blame, not me."

Rodheimer turned to a side table, leaving the image playing out on the wall, and he turned back with a series of photographs. He spread them on the desk.

Garik's aunt, Irina, and her boyfriend, Arik, coming out of Fasst Market, hand in hand, with Arik holding a plastic Fasst Market bag. Irina was smiling and she looked happy.

Another showed The Flower Shop, the back door, Marisa inserting a key. It seemed to be early morning with the long shadows, and Marisa wore a coat, gloves, and a bright scarf around her neck. Her cheeks were red with the cold.

Another of Hayat al-Haber in his headscarf and robe in the skate park on his sister's unicorn board.

And Muhammad, Ibn, even Mrs. Waggoner at City View Apartments, his upstairs neighbor.

"What's this?" Brace touched the photos, shifted them around.

"A way to get control. Give me time, Colonel. This worked once." Rodheimer tapped Marisa's image. "The boy will crack when we use what's important to him."

"We hardly have time." He lifted the picture of Marisa, studied it, then looked at Garik. "Pretty girl. You care about her? If so, we can see that she is happy, or—"

"Not yet, Colonel." Rodheimer slipped the paper from the man's hand and returned it to the table.

"The waterfront. We've yet to discuss that. We require access for our ships." Brace cut a hard eye to Garik, making it clear he would slice him like a tomato if he could, before returning his attention to Rodheimer.

Rodheimer touched his desk. The wall switched to show the events at the waterfront. "I have dispersed security to clean it up."

True enough, the men Garik had seen in the lobby—or ones very much the same—were doing what they could to get the chaos under control. It was hard to say if they would be successful. There were a lot of them, but there were more rioters, and the rioters didn't care what they damaged. Rodheimer seemed to treat it as manageable.

"I can offer more, if you need my help." Brace's statement was less an offer than a suggestion that he knew it was needed.

"This is my fight, Colonel." Rodheimer stacked up the photos, tapped them straight, and returned them to the side table.

"And my funds."

Garik didn't suppose the Colonel expected him to overhear that. He didn't think the man knew exactly what he was dealing with when it came to the hybrids in the Corona Tower basements.

And Garik knew one thing with an overwhelming confidence. He wasn't planning to be the one to tell him.

$$-\,8\,-$$

arik, released from Rodheimer's office under a raging storm cloud that had yet to discharge the torrent he still expected to flood the research center at any moment, was escorted back to the cafeteria through a lobby now devoid of humans, hybrids, and anyone who could claim anything resembling mutant fame.

The roving televisions were also gone, except for one that had been somehow shuffled into the cafeteria and overlooked. He found Devon and Kevin, to his amazement, still sitting at the same table with glasses of clear drinks and waiting on him. He threw himself into a third seat hard enough that he shifted the chair, bumped the table, and sloshed one of the glasses. Devon caught it just in time.

"Where's everyone?" He glanced around. Only one other person was present on the other side of the room with a plate of food, and she didn't look up.

"Back on schedule. Sunchaser came through and said we were wasting hours that could be put to better use. No one dared argue with her."

"You guys are here."

"Sunchaser instructed us to wait on you. We were under no account to let you out of our sight until Bay City was calm again."

"I bet. You think there's a war up there. I just got back from—"

"Not here." Devon leaned down as if to push a finger inside the top of his cast to scratch, and he hissed the words at him. When he raised up, he smiled. "Okay, kiddo, Kevin and I have decided you need to let off some steam. You've been babysitting me so well, you need some fun. We've cleared Kevin's schedule just for you. How does that sound? Pool, or something with a little more smash and bang?"

"I can smash and bang pretty well." Kevin grinned. "That's my specialty."

Garik looked from one man to the other. He understood. He was being hushed up, but down two floors, there were places they could talk freely without being overheard. And they wanted to know exactly what had happened while he was gone.

"Yeah, that would be fun, sure. I bet you can't touch me, Kevin-o."

"Watch it, Kev, the kid'll be doing that from now on if you don't stop him." Devon laughed, stood, and looked for his Segway. It was just inside the door by the lobby. "Garik, can you fetch my wheels, please?"

Garik also retrieved his ZBoard. Kevin walked. Devon had his passkey out, and they used it to get to Level 3. Garik needed time to process the meeting, so their plan was exercise first, then time in the pool. Heat up then cool off. Garik could reveal the details of his detention in the privacy of the changing rooms. To allow Devon to participate, they chose racquetball. Devon could serve, and the other two would continue the game. It gave them a valid reason to be on the training floor and together.

Garik found he was more worked up over the accusations lobbed at him by Rodheimer and Brace than he thought. He felt he had his emotions under control, not moving too fast, allowing Kevin plenty of good hits, and careful not to impact Devon, who didn't have the agility to avoid wild balls. But as the game went on, he found himself hitting harder, the ball blurring faster, and his companions more out of breath with each round. Finally, one ball left his racquet, impacted the front wall, and exploded with a loud pop, leaving a powdery stain where it had hit.

"Maybe it's time for the pool, kiddo. How about that?" Devon hobbled to him and grabbed his neck. He called to Kevin, who was panting with his hands on his knees, "See, Kev, I told you he was faster than he let on."

"But I won last time." Kevin stood, his face red, and sucking in air. "How did you manage to get so good today?"

Garik shrugged.

"I'm telling you, the kid's good at not giving away what he can do. Isn't that right, kiddo?" Devon slapped him on the back and called to Kevin, "My ride, James."

"Psst! Let Garik get it. I'm headed to the pool." Kevin dropped his racquet and grabbed the handle to the door.

"Leave it like you found it, huh?" Garik called after him. "Better if you can. Seems I heard that before."

"Grr. I should have tackled you before you reached that elevator. At least Marisa escaped. Now I have you to babysit." He did return to gather up his racket, and he also picked up two used towels from the floor.

"Lucky you." Garik grinned. When Kevin threw one of the towels at him, he caught it and threw it back. Then he ran to the front wall, picked up the remains of the burst ball, and pulled off his shirt to clean the wall.

By the time he returned, Devon was on the Segway, but Kevin had absconded with Garik's ZBoard. He shrugged, glad he was feeling better. He jogged to the natatorium, selected a suit and towel from the supply room, and disappeared under the water.

Several others were using the facility, but they were diving, and the lanes were uncrowded. Garik's practice sessions with Christian returned to him as soon as he hit the water, and he began holding his breath for longer and longer stretches. At one point, both Devon and Kevin were slapping the water to get his attention.

He broke the surface in the middle of the pool and called, "What?"

"Time!" Devon pointed to his watch. He was still clothed, but Kevin knelt on the side in his suit.

"You guys ready to go already?" Garik treaded water easily.

"No, come up for air once in a while. We thought you'd drowned."

"You mean I'm that good?" Garik laughed, dropped back under, and swam three more lengths before making his way to the side.

Devon had a waterproof board, and he marked a time on it. "I heard you were good underwater. No normal person can hold their breath that long."

"Am I missing something?" Garik grasped the side of the pool and swung himself up, landing on his feet, his skin a waterfall of wet. "Or are you? I'm not normal any longer. This place made sure of that."

Kevin shook his head and stood. "Are you blaming them for the sass, too? Bust a nickel. Let's get changed."

In the changing rooms, with their towels tossed to the side and fresh clothes on, Garik confirmed, "No microphones, right, Dev-o?"

"Shouldn't be. Except for the training cells, this is about as private as it gets down here."

"As long as Justin's not around, right?" Justin Kurtew had rigged one months before. Devon had removed it and monitored the place regularly.

"Right-o, kiddo. So, what happened with the Director?"

Revealing the accusations cut him. Colonel Brace enjoyed twisting the Director's accusations just to make them bleed. Anger surged in him, but it wasn't Devon or Kevin at fault, and more than once, he had to pause and repeat his old internal mantra: *Anger gets me nothing. I must use my hands, my mind, my desire to achieve.*

They were exiting the elevator on Level 2 when red lights on the wall began to flash. The corridor leading to Corona City was a bric-a-brac shambles of spooked people. Stephen Klandermans and Paul Gberie ran toward them.

"What's with the excitement?" Devon waved and pulled them in.

"You people been hiding in a closet?" Stephen with his kinky blond dreadlocks and tattered clothes yelled to them as he slowed.

"You people been on the elevator." Paul's laugh revealed his gold-inset teeth. His skin flickered in random pulses of orange, revealing his high level of excitement. "Up into the real world, and welcome!"

"Have they cancelled the training sessions?" Kevin checked his watch. "I have several scheduled for later."

"Then you haven't heard. The Air Force is being booted out. If they're outside now, they can't return, and Rodheimer has security forcing those inside to pack their things and leave. He's already set up guards at the gate to the parking garage to keep them out."

"He can't keep them out," Garik blurted. "They'll come in—"

Devon elbowed him in the ribs, shutting him up and rewording his sentence. "They'll come in using the main elevator."

"He's put guards there, too. Everyone's trying to find out what's going on. You, Kevin, they're locking down the underground garage. If you're parked there, you'd better move your car while you can."

"I'm not. Besides, this is exciting! I'm the luckiest person in the world to be down here."

Garik thought of Lt. Miyoshi, part of the Air Force. She had been nice to him, and Airman Wu, who had bonded with him over his Street Strider. Others he didn't mind being kicked out, but not everyone deserved to be booted onto the street. He also wondered if this meant the back exit through the parking garage was sealed off. It was his only hope, even if he wasn't sure how he could access it.

The red lights flashed several times, visible at intervals along the corridors, with a short burp of a siren in between. A voice announced, "All military personnel must exit the facility. Things left behind will be inaccessible until further notice." The lights flashed once more.

It was a mystery that no one was bothering to explain.

LANSANA Opoku-Mensah, Veronika Abbink, and Zekeria Salem joined Stephen, Paul, Devon, Kevin, and Garik in Devon's apartment. Armor, color-changing skin, night vision, bone regeneration, a cloak of invisibility, a broken leg, a martial arts expert, and a teen who didn't know yet what he might become.

The big surprise came when Anatoli Burgorski and his brother Andrey knocked on the door. They brought in a white box about a meter square. Louise King followed with a small package in her hand.

"Garik," Devon began, pulling him to the center of the living room, while Anatoli, Andrey, and Louise gathered out of sight in the kitchen, "I wonder if you remember what day this is."

"Not really." He'd been knocked out for weeks, put through strenuous tests, not allowed access to the Internet, hospitalized more than once, and generally kept away from anything connected with the outside world. Even Christmas had slipped by unnoticed in this underground world without seasons or holidays.

"This is not possible, and we will not allow it." Veronika, with her large earrings, reached for her messenger bag, pulled out a giant envelope, and with a smile showing off her oversized teeth, turned it to reveal Garik's name.

"What's that for?" Garik's heart raced. There was only one thing this could be. How had he not remembered? Could he be eighteen *today*?

"What do you think Kevin and I talked about in the cafeteria for so long? Your good looks?" Devon laughed. "Not on your life. I do have access to your records with all kinds of good stuff." Devon motioned, and everyone turned to see a birthday cake on the counter with eighteen blazing candles. "I've wanted to tell you all day."

As everyone began singing, Garik's eyes filled with tears. He didn't even bother trying to wipe them away.

— 9 —

Good times are meant to be enjoyed, especially when there's every likelihood they can't last.

The people offering Garik best wishes on his eighteenth knew how to enjoy themselves. Stimulants did nothing for them, except bring back memories of good times from the past—a byproduct of their updated DNA—but that didn't keep them from being creative about other ways to have fun. Prankstering, good jokes, the unexpected application of their hybridized skills that were unique to them and them alone.

Armored coating? "Come on," Lansana taunted. "All knives welcome." If she was hit, it didn't matter. However, she was certain she wouldn't be.

Dancing skin? Paul pranced to a throbbing musical number, and his skin pulsed with designs to make a kaleidoscope slink away in shame.

Pranks in the dark? Zekeria proved he was the master, slipping in and out of shadows and startling everyone.

Kevin slammed Stephen to the floor over and over in martial arts moves that might kill other men. Stephen stood each time, unbroken and inviting more.

Even Garik got into it, blurring the world around him into a bevy of rainbows. He rearranged shirts on the men, shoes on the women, and if they had food to eat, switched out their plates and beverages. He was back in his chair, his muscles quivering, before the first person exclaimed, "What happened to my shirt?"

Kevin took the couch that night. Of course, Devon was in his bed, and Garik tumbled under the covers in his own room, not even closing the door, and only slightly wishing his old friends—Ibn, Muhammad, Marisa, and the others—could have been at his party. He then could have eaten a salty biscuit, jumped over a bonfire, and danced with a girl. It was what he had looked forward to in his early years in Russia. He wondered what his aunt might have given him for turning from a boy to a man. That's what the evening had been, a celebration of putting off his short pants and slipping on trousers for the first time.

He pulled his blanket to his chest and traced the corners of his ceiling. It no longer seemed strange to be able to easily follow the lines in the dark, or to count the recessed fixtures, or to make out every item of furniture in the otherwise darkened space.

He closed his eyes, content in the moment. Houdini time could wait until morning. For one night, he had good dreams to keep him company.

GARIK'S DREAMS were barely an hour old—not even adolescent status when you compared the eight hours a person dreamed to the eighty years of a person's life—when pounding at the apartment door jerked him awake.

"Open up!" The pounding started again, more insistent this time.

"Coming!" Kevin's voice.

Something fell off a table and shattered, then light from the living room tumbled through Garik's door. He pushed himself up on his elbows. His eyes burned at the searing brightness.

The door unlocked, thump, thump, a familiar sound, and a gruff voice stated, "Take this. List everyone inside. Your door is being manually disengaged. If you try to exit, you will be shot. Keep the list by the door.

We'll be by in the morning to retrieve it."

The door slammed and locked, thump, thump, and Garik swung his legs to the floor and called, "Kevin?"

The man wandered in, disheveled, and held out a sheet of paper. "Here, they left this. Let me get the light." Kevin stumbled on Garik's shoe and said, "Ow, are you trying to kill me?"

"I can see fine."

"You have better eyes than I do. Have it your way. I don't mind the dark."

Garik took the paper and recognized it as a type of census. The top said NONCOMBATANTS, and there were lines for names and other information, some of it in small print.

"So, who gave you this?"

"Some guy in black."

"Riot control?" Garik pictured the people from the lobby earlier. They had been headed out to the city to squash the rabble and bring them under control.

"Nah, different. Their helmets had gas mask things, and there were these symbols on their sleeves, like an eagle in a circle. Do what you want with that. I'm back to bed. Nite."

Kevin left, leaving Garik with the form. When the light in the other room went out, it really was too dark to read, so Garik set it on the side table and slipped back under the covers. The form might say noncombatant, but it wasn't protection. It was tabulation.

People added to it wouldn't be excused from the fighting if it came to that.

Devon hobbled in some time later, his cast only partially covered by one pajama leg that had been sliced open. "Hey, kiddo, do you have that form?"

"Sure." He was awake instantly. He'd been caught up in a battle between Weston Rodheimer and Colonel Brace, and Halo Sunchaser had just appeared with her blazing sword sending lightning everywhere. He was ready to be done with that. He reached to the bedside for the form and held it out.

"Garik, the form?" Devon remained at the door.

"Right. You normal people need light to see." He meant it as a joke, not realizing how true it was. He hit the switch, and the lamp beside the bed clicked on.

"Thanks. Sorry for not waking up. I took something for the leg and didn't hear anything." He made his way to the end of the bed and sat. He didn't have his crutches, and he braced his fall with his hands. He straightened the form and read it over. "So, the Colonel wins."

"What?"

Devon handed him the form, and this time, Garik absorbed it, even the small print. It even provided scheduled times for each apartment for each meal of the day. They would have a military escort every time they left the apartment.

A rising tide of dismay in Garik yelled, "No, no,

no!" He was supposed to escape. The secret exit was his plan. If the Tower and the basement research campus were now the military's domain, what good was Houdini? He could be locked in a trunk and cast adrift, for all the good he was, and he would likely drown.

He wished for his birthday celebration back again. For one night he had held something good, and now, it was taken away again. They couldn't let him have eighteen, not even for a full day. How crummy was that?

BREAKFAST REVEALED the true scale of the disaster.

Two unfamiliar goons in new and different attire showed up at their door, their faces covered, and their voices filtered through circular masks elongating their chins. They could have been the true mutants, for all the humanity they revealed through their black chiton shells. They took the form, looked at the three names, and passed it from one to the other.

"Two normals and one half-human. Who's the half?"

Garik raised his hand.

"Okay. You look normal enough that we need to mark you. Hold out your left hand."

Garik looked to Kevin and Devon, but he knew they had no say in this situation, and he gritted his teeth and did as the man asked. He watched him clip on a bright orange band and tug it tight. The man tested it, satisfied it wouldn't come off, and motioned the three of them to follow.

Sentries stood at every corner with weapons strapped over their shoulders or at their side. Equipment belts, heavy boots, helmets, with the white on black logo stamped everywhere. Not regular military, Garik stored away, after they passed the fifth one. There was no cafeteria on Level 2, so it was no surprise to have the masked strangers press Level 1 in the elevator.

There was evidence of a struggle during the night. Scorched places littered the floor like scattered clumps of windblown paper. From the outside, one of the elevator doors on Level 1 didn't match the other. One of the exotic modern sculptures had been reworked with a hail of gunfire, and it was more hole than sculpture. Garik wondered who had been hiding there, and if they had made their escape.

Other residents were also being escorted to the cafeteria, but all were being kept apart. Even inside, no two occupied tables were next to each other. Food was brought to them by one of the kitchen staff. They weren't asked what they wanted, so clearly, there was no point in requesting something special.

Those eating had either one or two guards at their side. One for a single person, two for groups of two or three. No table had more than two guards, so it was a bit of a surprise when a third goon guard walked up, gave an awkward salute, and spoke to the two who had escorted them from Devon's apartment.

"The hybrid needs to come with me." Like the two earlier, his voice had a filtered sound, odd but not unlike a real person's.

"The half-human, you mean." The guard pulled his gun from his shoulder and tapped the bracelet at Garik's wrist, as if to touch him was to "get" his hybrid disease.

"Just him. He needs to come with me. The Colonel needs to see him."

"Good enough. You're welcome to it."

It? Garik felt his blood heat up. He was a *him*. A *person*. Captured and *forced* to become what he was. No one had asked him, no one said if you please, and he didn't appreciate being called an *it*.

Before he could go off on the man, the new guard rapped the table with his knuckles and said, "Garik, if you please."

That got Garik's attention, the way the man said his name, as if he knew him. That gravelly voice, even through the suit, seemed . . . no, and Garik shook his head. Wishful thinking got him nowhere, and he stood.

"Devon, Kevin, if I don't return, you, Devon, can have all my pajamas. Put them on, please. And Kevin, I want you to have my ZBoard. Ride it with spirit." He grinned, then wiped it from his face and turned to the guard. He held out his wrists. "Handcuffs?"

"Not likely," the man's voice growled. "Let's move it. No time like now."

They moved toward the corridor leading to the underground parking garage. The damage was greater, leading Garik to think this was where the research complex had been compromised. An opening where there used to be a door; shattered glass; blackened places where things had burned.

Once they were completely out of view of everyone else, his guard said, "Whew! This is exhausting." Then, he melted into a more familiar shape, or at least his head and hands did. His beaded clothing took a second longer to change from eagle soldier to rescuing friend, making Paul whole.

"Paul?" Garik wanted to whoop. "What's the plan?"

"Wondering if you want to go for a ride." Colors rippled over the man's face, riddled with yellow for humor and interspersed with orange for excitement. He pulled out a key fob from his beaded robe and held it for Garik to see.

At voices from just ahead, Paul grabbed Garik's wrist to cover the bright orange band and held a finger to his lips. "Shush," and his color and shape transformed into the military goon from minutes before. His clothing took a bit longer and made the change just before the men rounded the corner.

"Sirs," Paul said in his filtered, gravelly voice, as he pushed Garik to the wall and out of their way. He offered a salute as the men passed.

"Take care, soldier. At ease." The men nodded but didn't salute back.

When they burst into the garage, to the right, the access from the old parking garage on Stamford was brilliantly lighted. The aboveground garage was gone, and the ramp now led to open air.

What was better was far in the distance. A portion of the north wall of the garage—the back entrance!—was no longer secret. To judge by the damage, that was how the military had gained access. Olive-drab trucks and other transports filled the underground, and black-suited men were everywhere. Several vehicles waited to head out, as one rumbled in.

Paul pushed the fob, and an ordinary black SUV with tinted windows flashed its lights and beeped.

"They won't let us out in that." They needed to pretend to be military if they intended to escape.

"Trust me. They'll let us through."

Garik turned to argue, only to find he was standing at Colonel Brace's side.

— 10 —

olonel, sir."

A big man in a black suit with the eagle logo on his upper arm stepped to them and saluted. He carried his helmet, as though he had just removed it and might have need to put it on again. The air in the garage was warm near the elevator but colder near the two exposed exits. Neither Paul nor Garik was dressed for the cold.

"Yes, um, Rodrigo." Paul cleared his throat, not sounding very much like the colonel but giving it his best "military" voice. He glanced up from the man's name on his uniform. "I need to take the, um, hybrid with me. We have, um, business to take care of. Thank you."

If Garik weren't so nervous that they would be exposed as imposters—rather that Paul would be exposed, as it was clear who he was—he would have found Paul's attempts to mimic Colonel Brace as a good game, but not a very successful one. Apparently, to their good luck, Rodrigo accepted Paul's stuttered impersonation without much thought.

"I saw your truck unlock, sir. Let me get you a driver." The man was already looking across the garage for an available man. Paul as Brace stopped him.

"Thank you, Rodrigo. I need to do this on my own. It can be our little secret." Paul winked.

Garik's heart dropped when he saw the wink, prepared for the soldier to sound the alarm and for the handcuffs to come out. Winking was something Brace would not do in a million years.

"If you're sure, sir. Understand that things have gotten much worse since we broke through last night." He pulled a paper map of Bay City from a back pocket and a thick-tipped marker from another. He walked to Brace's SUV and spread the paper map on the hood. "These streets are a no-go, sir." He placed bold X marks on them. "To get out, you need to take a right on Lowell. Left is obstructed. At Scenic, you can go either direction. If you can give me a destination, I can radio ahead to ensure your safety." He traced the short route to Scenic Drive in a bold stroke.

"Um," and Paul glanced at Garik, who mouthed, Argyle Station, and said, "The Argyle, um, Station? Yes, that's where we need to go. I'm, um, meeting someone."

"Are you sure, sir?" Rodrigo frowned. "The trains haven't run all night. Whoever you're meeting isn't likely to be there now."

"No, I mean, yes, I understand, er, know that. How could I not know that? I am the Colonel, after all." He nodded awkwardly. "I expect he, er, they will still be there. From the last train, I mean, before things were, shall we say, interrupted."

"Are you sure you don't want me to get you a driver, sir?" Rodrigo looked from Paul, whom he had been studying intently, to Garik and the orange band on his arm. Then he relaxed. "Ah, this is the boy from the protests. I understand. Negotiations. If anyone asks, you weren't here."

"Thank you, Rodrigo. We'll be off, now."

"The map, sir?" Rodrigo folded it twice and held it out.

"Of course. Wouldn't want to run into a roadblock and get stopped."

"No sir." The man glared at Garik, as if he were the reason for all this nonsense that was happening to Bay

City.

Perhaps he was, Garik considered, as he walked around the truck to the passenger's side. Even so, that didn't mean it was his *fault*. Blame Dr. Jimenez. Put the onus on Weston Rodheimer. Take aim at Halo Sunchaser with your blame machine. When you fire, you might also lob your accusations onto Colonel Brace, and maybe a few others who liked to stand too close.

Paul, as Colonel Brace, started the black truck, and he shifted into gear. The darkened windows gave them a sense of separation from the military anthill around them, but they weren't out yet. The gauntlet had just begun.

RODRIGO UNWITTINGLY made their escape easier than pie. He rapped the hood of the big vehicle once they were inside, lifted his left arm, and stretched it toward the ragged hole where the back entrance used to hide. He motioned Paul forward and walked with him as he instructed others to move out of the way.

Closer to the exit, the man held his hand up for them to hold, and he navigated the line waiting to exit the garage. As one big truck shifted into reverse and forced another truck to pull out of the way, Rodrigo reached in his helmet, placed a clear breathing mask on an extendable tube to his face and drew in a deep breath. He returned the mask to his helmet and motioned Paul and Garik forward. Approaching the exit, the massive automotive elevator that would have dropped vehicles below the street level to access the dummy office building across the street dropped down ten feet beside them, exposing part of the concrete tunnel running under the street. A blackened troop transport, crushed, rested half on and half off the elevator and suggested it might not be operational again anytime soon. Garik hoped no one had died, but the transport had clearly been allowed to burn itself out. That explained the new hole in the wall opening directly to Lowell.

Rodrigo saluted, and Paul eased the vehicle into the morning sunshine. A slight haze filled the air, adding a subtle otherworldliness to the scene, and the sun glinted off scattered patches of snow. The dummy building across the street with the painted windows and false bushes jumped out at Garik. Whoever had constructed it had done well. Without knowing what he knew now, there was nothing to differentiate it from any normal building in Bay City. No wonder no one knew its real use.

Left, as Rodrigo had suggested, no one was getting through. A large panel truck was overturned with goods scattered across the roadway. Intentional? Garik couldn't tell. A team of black suits was in the process of clearing one lane, and a crane was setting up to put the panel truck back on its wheels.

They were almost to Scenic Drive when Paul

resolved back into himself. His skin rippled, pulsing with finding his original shape once again and finally settled into his true features. He grinned, flashing his gold-inlaid teeth.

"Well, that went better than I expected. That was a long time to be an evil man. Better me than him."

Garik scanned the marshlands past Scenic. To the left, ten blocks away, Harbor Shipyards dominated the horizon. Normally, he would expect to see gantry cranes and giant trucks moving about, with sparks flying as welders attached this to that to build the biggest and best ships on the West Coast. Smoke rose ominously from the end of one of the giant warehouses, and the whole end was collapsed and blackened. Everywhere else, the Shipyards was devoid of life. The Docks wasn't visible from this end of Lowell, but he had seen the television screens. It was unlikely anything was getting in or out from there.

Garik glanced at Paul, taking in his large lips and dusky skin, noting the feminine cast of his profile but thinking nothing of it. He was trying to overlay the colonel's features, and even the soldier goon's from before that on the jokster's face.

"Aren't you afraid your teeth will give you away?"

"Me?" Paul laughed. "How many times did you see me smile?"

"None, I guess."

"No guess. I am pretty smart up here." He tapped

his forehead. The big SUV pulled up to the light at Lowell and Scenic Drive, and Paul asked, "To Argyle Station, correct? Right or left?"

"You're asking me? I thought you had a plan."

"No plan. The keys, that's what I brought to our little escape. They came available, and I said to myself, Paul, that boy needs your help. He will be chopped into tiny pieces. How can you allow that? So, I borrowed them, and here we are. You, my friend, must have a plan, otherwise—" He shrugged broadly.

"We're not going to Argyle Station. I'm not empty-headed, either. That was a distraction."

"Ah, smart boy." Paul laughed hard for a moment. "Now, I can only say *man* because you blew out all the candles on the cake. No more do I have a little boy sitting in the car with me, true?"

"Turn right." Garik turned his head, irritated, and looked out his window. He hadn't been a *boy* since before getting entangled with the Tower, and he certainly wasn't one now.

"Is all in good fun, heh?" Paul reached over and pushed on Garik's shoulder.

"Stop it," Garik said, tucking in against the door.

"Stop it," Paul repeated.

"Hey," Garik threw out, turning to find himself riding with Charlotte Mnich. "Stop. Be yourself. I don't like not knowing who I'm with."

"So be it." Paul's voice was as gravelly as ever,

telling the truth of who he was, and he let his body shift to match his true form. "We must go somewhere, and we must get there soon. The keys, someone will miss them, and we do not want to be discovered."

"Right, right." Garik tried to process. Right on Scenic would eventually take them out of town, but the forested area to the east of Bay City was undeveloped, and he didn't know the lay of the land, except what he'd seen on maps. He had friends in the city, though he had no easy way to contact them. Jantzen and the team that had escaped with him before might still be in Bay City. They would help him hide.

And now he had Paul to consider. Would he fit neatly into that group of friends? Or would their shared experiences exclude Paul except as an unwelcome and abrasive sticker in their side? He seemed to find satisfaction in turning over rocks to see what crawled out.

The light changed, and Garik motioned to the right. Paul turned and accelerated. Here, there was little to suggest Bay City was in an uproar and the military was stepping in to quell unrest and exert control over the rioters. The marshy floodlands to the left and glimpses through the bare trees of the large estates to the right revealed a normal scene untouched by the protesters.

At Park Avenue, Garik again pointed right. He didn't have a destination, but south was what he knew. The high school, Central Park, the police headquarters, the skate park, and even the Ransom Building, although that wasn't even remotely on his options list. They had erased that place the first night he and Jantzen Hefferly had escaped using Kevin Lee's van. It could never be used as a safe house again.

His sense of right and wrong was shifted off its foundation when they passed Bay City High. A banner covered the name on the front of the building and proclaimed it BCA Tactical Staging. The parking lot was filled with military trucks, and the sports fields revealed soldiers involved in training exercises. An unfamiliar flag fluttered on the flagpole, one with a stylized eagle superimposed against a black background.

"That's not Air Force." The knowledge was a flood in Garik's mind. "They're not real military at all."

"Para," Paul stated, his word empty of inflection. "You saw the emblem. The eagle in the circle."

"Yes, but—" Garik considered his "but." He had seen it and considered it another level of military, not paramilitary. They were no more than hired thugs. At least that's the way he pictured them. "They are working with our military."

"That's what paramilitary does, least if they're on our side, and I hope these are. I don't think Colonel Brace liked losing, so he took whatever steps were needed to make sure he didn't."

Passing Central Park, the black-faced goons were working the park side-by-side with the real military's camouflage green. The goons held the weapons, and the camouflage green walked along, seeing that the people who had decimated the park policed their own trash and other garbage. Even the tents were mostly gone. Garik was sure they would be by dark.

The duck pond was still lined with trash, likely carried in by the wind. He watched a duck land, oblivious, and dip its head underwater as if searching for food.

Now that he was paying attention, he had no trouble seeing the difference between the Tower's black goons and Brace's equally black goons. These goons were bigger, wider, and more ominous than the Tower security forces had ever been. If that wasn't a giveaway, the masks they wore painted them as mean as they looked.

Except for seeing Rodrigo's face, Garik could easily believe they weren't human at all.

That's when the light came on. Perhaps they were like him, half human, only designed to be bigger, better, and more powerful than any normal man could be . . . only their kind had received a hybrid-induced flaw. That would explain the masks.

"Pull over, now," he insisted. Before Paul could stop the truck, Garik had the door open, and he let his breakfast fly.

— II —

he statue in the small park across from police headquarters was toppled over. Where it lay in the grass, it
was decorated with spray-painted words that extended
onto the base. Garik read aloud, "Let the—" and his
eyes skipped from the toppled statue for the rest, "—
boy go."

"And now they have." Paul laughed and popped
him lightly in the chest with the back of his hand. "Bet
Brace never saw me coming, you think?"

They continued to navigate destruction, including parked cars with windows punched in or graffiti on the sides, and one with its nose jammed through a storefront. People wrapped against the cold turned and watched as they passed, a few dropping to hide, and others remaining blatantly in the open, as if daring the black SUV to challenge them in their fight to reclaim Bay City for the people.

Garbage bins overflowed, revealing the lack of trash pickup, and there was more scattered along the curbs and sidewalks, giving this part of Park an abandoned, apocalyptic feel. Where the black-suited goons with the paramilitary eagles hadn't intervened, violent-looking crowds swarmed, lemmings all, and off the cliff we go.

Even the police station had graffiti scrawled on one wall, a message that blasted, "Tower Owned and Operated." One window was covered with plywood, and the brickwork just underneath was blackened as though an explosive cocktail had tried to burn the building down.

Garik wondered if he would recognize anyone he knew. Coats, scarves, the sheer volume of protesters. They could be hidden behind any number of things, even abandoned cars, mounds of garbage, or simply a passing street sign. He would have no idea.

At Third Street, something high in the sky caught his attention. He followed it and grinned. "Paul, turn right on the next street."

"Oka-ay. Whatever you say, boss." He hit the

brakes and turned at a faster clip than the big SUV appreciated. The backend skipped and slid before falling in line. Away from Park, the damage from the rioting was left behind. Within the first block, the residue remaining from the riots was mostly windblown trash, and of course, the garbage bins that waited to be emptied. Paul asked, "Now where?"

"Hold on. I'm tracking it." Garik leaned forward, watching out the windshield. "Slow down. I don't want to lose it."

He was about to, anyway, and he rolled down his window and pulled himself out to sit on the window ledge. He braced himself using the mirror and the top of the door. The air was cold, but he needed to be sure before giving Paul additional instructions.

"There, Paul. Right on Douglas. Now, this street."

The truck jerked Garik against the doorframe, smashing the edge into his chest. He held on until the vehicle righted itself. The City Transportation Department covered the entire city block to their left. It didn't look like any city transportation stuff was happening today, probably closed with the rest of the city over the ensuing riots. Through a substantial fence, backhoes, a dump truck, and several snowplows nestled in the remains of a snowstorm that had come and gone without Garik getting to enjoy it. Several smaller vehicles were covered, the edges of gray tarps held down with large concrete blocks peeking out of their snowy grave.

Garik began waving with both arms, and Paul hit him on the leg.

"We're trying to hide, not give ourselves away."

"I see someone I know." He yelled, "Justin!"

"Kurtew?" Paul hit the brakes hard, sending the map into the floor and Garik nearly to the ground. "Where?"

"In the sky." Garik had to make sure Justin saw him. He forced himself through the window and dropped to the pavement. He ran in front of the truck and jumped up and down and waved his arms.

Far overhead, a winged shape hovered for a minute, then began to drop. The wings were there because Garik knew they must be, but they were more blurred sky than visible wings. Justin, however, was unmistakable, with his long torso, the extra joints in his arms, and his head that was more insect-like than ever. Garik called again, and Justin waved and fell like a stone to gingerly alight on the street a short distance away. His wings slowed, became visible, but continued to flutter, as if he were ready to return aloft at the first opportunity.

"Justin!" Garik started his direction when the man's wings blurred, and he lifted from the ground. He called, "Wait!"

"Why is Brace here?" Justin clacked his teeth, his jaw more beak than mouth.

"He's not. I escaped. I hoped to find someone—"

"That's Brace's truck." Justin's hands whirred, and he held two knives, from where, who knew? He still hovered just above the roadway tarmac. "Brace must know, we won't go back."

"Hey, loser!" The SUV's door opened, and Paul stepped out, his hands in the air, only it was Jantzen Hefferly, with his dark hair and beard, and his piercing, purple-flecked eyes.

"I don't think so." One of Justin's hands blurred, and a knife blade was buried in the metal of the door. "Another lie and I won't miss."

"Have it your way." Paul shifted into his true shape, and he walked forward, exposing himself to whatever Justin wanted to do. "Haven't seen the wings. Impressive, you loser, you. Come on down and give me a hug."

"Paul Gberie." Justin's feet settled on the pavement. "So, you become Brace, and you drive away with no repercussions. And you secret out Garik at the same time."

"Well, some repercussions." He leaned over and touched the blade of the knife where it pierced the door. "And they know Garik's with me. We're on an errand for a secret meeting to negotiate with the protesters to make all this go away."

"What?" Justin's wings blurred, and he was once more aloft. His second knife hovered in an outstretched hand, and it was clear someone might die.

"No, Justin! Don't throw it." Garik turned to Paul. "Be serious for one minute. Sheesh!"

"Explain," Justin commanded.

Garik took charge. "That's what the soldier thought, that we were going to Argyle Station to negotiate with me as the prize. They get me, and Colonel Brace gets the city back."

"No one is at Argyle Station. No trains have run for days." Justin's hand hadn't wavered.

"I know, Justin, and so does Paul." Garik wanted to yank the man from the sky. He could beat him at whatever he wanted to try. He'd proved that, but what he needed was Justin's cooperation . . . and for Paul to quit poking the anthill just to see the ants run. "It was a ruse, a secret negotiation that he couldn't reveal. We hoped it would give us more time."

"I see." Justin touched down again. "If true, only partly successful. I have been tracking this truck, assuming it was Brace. There are others on the way."

"We thought as much." Paul's face rippled with laughter. "We need to hide. Can you help?"

"Agreed. Hiding is paramount. You are already being tracked by Brace's men. We know about the reinforcements from Canada. They appear to be as fearsome as suggested."

As suggested? Garik's ears perked up. So, Justin knew about the upgraded men. He wondered what else the man knew.

"Is anyone else with you?"

"Just us chickens."

Garik turned to glare at Paul only to see a man-sized chicken standing in the street. "Stop it, Paul," he demanded. "Sheesh! You're worse than a twelve-year-old. No, Justin," he called. "No one else is with us. Check if you want."

"Thank you." His wings stilled, and he folded them at his back. With a rocking gait, he moved toward the truck, peered inside, and nodded. With a flash of his wrist, the knife disappeared. "We will move the truck into the lot and cover it. There it will be safe."

A wide gate began to roll sideways, the wheels rumbling on their tracks, the chain-driven sound of welcome already gathering them in.

TWO PEOPLE appeared from behind the rolling gate. Joanie McDonald, once sporting a bold mohawk, now had a knit beanie pulled tightly over her ears. She was wrapped against the cold in a thick, quilted coat.

"Peach Fuzz," she called with a wave.

"Joanie!" Garik grinned.

The second was John Carter. His larger-than-life torso was covered only with a thin tee. Once the gate got rolling, he took over and shooed Joanie away.

John called, "Paul, pull that truck in before we get drones overhead searching for it."

"Johnnie boy," Paul called. "Missed you, friend."

John snorted. "Just pull in the lot. We'll talk about the friend part later."

Paul grinned and climbed in. He rolled down the window, reached out, worked the knife back and forth until it came loose, and he tossed it Justin's direction. The man's hand blurred, and he held it. It blurred again, and the knife disappeared.

Once inside, John pulled a tarp off one of the city vehicles, and he, Paul, and Garik worked it over the SUV and secured it with four of the concrete blocks.

"Are we safe here?" This was a city building, and Garik remembered how quickly the Tower had found them at the Ransom Communications Building. They had triggered sensors, and the Tower had sent forces to retrieve them within hours.

"Not to worry," Justin assured him. "This way."

Once inside, Garik saw what he meant. The side of the building facing Douglas was undamaged. They hadn't driven past the McKinley Street side. They found the front of a commercial truck buried in the façade, and the hood and one axle protruded into the room.

"It shorted the power to the entire building. We have a generator for lights but use propane for heat." John nodded at Garik and Paul. "Bet you're glad for that."

"Sure. Where's everyone else?" Paolo Leveen, Alyna Lindberg, the others.

"Just the three of us," Joanie answered. "Come." They entered a machine shop, also set up as a makeshift living space. She pulled off her cap to reveal little more than fuzz on her head.

"They cut your hair?" Garik was used to her towering mohawk, and he remembered the first time he woke in the Tower's basements and learned that they had shorn his completely off. He had been devastated. It was only now growing out to what it used to be.

"Better that than this." She dropped into a chair and didn't elaborate.

"Part of the reason we're here and not out there," John said. "Can I tell him, Joanie?"

"Knock yourself out." She waved a hand to brush away the question.

"Joanie has had to regenerate—"

"It works?" Garik lit up with excitement. He knew exactly what he meant. That was Joanie's supposed skill from her jellyfish DNA. It had never been tested. She would have to be killed—or nearly—to check it, and not even the Tower had wanted to risk that. Then the other side of what must have happened dropped him to a chair. "Then you were—" He couldn't say it.

"Yah, about," she said. "You got it, Peach Fuzz," and she drew one finger across her throat.

"I'm sorry." Garik had seen Justin's transformation when he had molted to get his wings. He tried to imagine what regenerating from death might be like, and he couldn't.

"Hey, got something you might be interested in." John pulled up a chair to a desk and slipped a keyboard from a drawer. He turned it on, and on the wall above the desk, a large screen flickered on. John typed in some instructions, and a room appeared on the other side. They could see the back of someone's head and that there were other people present but not who. John called, "Amy. Turn around."

Amy Howe shifted her position, and the petite woman smiled. "John! What do you need?"

"Look who's with me." He motioned Garik over.

"Garik!" Amy's face lit up. Then someone pushed her aside.

"Garik? Move over, Amy. Garik, is that really you?" Marisa's face filled the screen.

It was the happiest moment of Garik's day, and he couldn't wipe the smile from his face.

— 12 —

y apologies, Garik, but we don't dare keep the line open." John turned from the darkened screen, and he slipped the keyboard back into the drawer. "I was certain you would want to know she is okay, and for her to see you, well, you saw her face light up. Knowing you're free did that for her."

"Still, we barely got to speak." They had said hello and I've missed you, and little more when Amy broke in and said she had to sever the connection.

"This bolt hole is only safe as long as we keep it safe. The Tower hasn't let go of us so easily. Joanie's the truth of that."

"Can we go where they are? That's safe, surely. If they're there, we can be there, or she can come here." To have seen Marisa, to be out of the Tower, to have all his nights dreaming of her so close he could touch, how could he not? It was so simple.

"Not so simple." Joanie rapped the table with her knuckles.

Garik looked at her as if she had read his mind. Maybe she had. Had anyone ever studied if jellyfish could do that? Maybe they could, and people had never thought of it, and it took Joanie's DNA being combined with jellyfish DNA to find out.

"It *is* simple. Paul and I got here. We can get to where Marisa's at as easily. Paul has a good disguise, better than maybe any of us, and I can move really fast. We won't get caught."

"Seriously," Justin confirmed. His eyes seemed clouded by something dark, but then, had Garik ever seen him happy or cheerful? "Not so simple. We divided into four teams, and we haven't shared the locations."

"But, you must need to talk to one another, plan—"

"That." He pointed to the large monitor.

"For more than two minutes, I hope." It reminded him of the research center's rules. Do it this way or that way because that's what the rules said. Well, he was tired of the rules.

"Not even for two minutes." John glanced at the dark screen. "It's why we couldn't let you and Marisa say much to one another. If the line happens to be tapped, too many verbal clues might lead them to us. No, we use it to set up drop-offs. In code, of course. No one wants to show up at a drop off and discover a team of Tower bullies there to apprehend us."

"You go out to the drop offs? How is that better? You are just as exposed." This sounded like another convoluted way to keep him and Marisa apart.

"Only Justin for us. He flies. Each team has some-one who's especially suited for reconnaissance and retrieval."

Julia Cantos came to mind. DNA merged with a boa constrictor meant she could sense body heat with uncanny accuracy. When people were too far away to sense her, she already knew they were there and likely their body weight and gender.

Of course, Amy. Her leafcutter bee DNA had given her hyperfine hair all over her body, and the simple shifting of air pressure or temperature was enough that she could avoid all but dead people, and she could usually find them, too. She would have no trouble out and across the city.

The final piece of the puzzle had to be Marco Lopez. He looked less human than the others, but with his lemur DNA's climbing ability and his tail for balance, he could travel routes that would shatter the confidence of parkour enthusiasts.

"You, Justin," Garik said, noting the names he'd come up with, "and Julia, Amy, and Marco, right?'

"Well, yes. How did you—"

"They are the only ones who could. The rest have useful fighting skills, but to navigate without being caught? It's obvious who you'd pick." Anyone could see it. "And Jantzen, no one's said anything about him. I would have put him as reconnaissance, but we know Jantzen."

John looked at Joanie and grinned. Justin's face grew even darker than it already was. Garik wondered what hold Jantzen had over Justin and why the other two were amused by him.

He also had a splinter of doubt, firmly driven in by Weston Rodheimer, that Jantzen had his own agenda in helping Garik and the other hybrids to escape. Where was he now?

Or was Jantzen being excluded because he might double-cross everyone?

It was something he couldn't resolve, and he didn't want to create tension by bringing it up now. Instead, he said, "How much do you know about what's happened in the Tower since yesterday?"

They wanted to know it all.

GARIK WAS astonished to learn that the new hybrids he'd befriended were all known to them. It shouldn't have surprised him. When he and Paul first encountered Justin in the street, Paul had barbed Justin, and Justin had replied in kind, if with a barb that was a bit more pointed and deadly than Paul's verbal jabs.

They just hadn't run together in the research center. They were divided by skills or backgrounds or potential usefulness to the program, or as in the case of those who had escaped with Jantzen, their lack of potential in the program. Tractability, or willingness to work with the military authority in power over the program, was a vital requirement in defining a candidate's potential. No matter the skills, if you weren't willing to bend your morals and goals to Colonel Brace's, you were shuffled down and down and finally out.

Garik wondered at a few of the hybrids he'd met, why they were still in the program. Paul, even, while Garik was glad he had disregarded Brace's authority to help him escape, had a distinct flair for carelessness with people and a disregard for authority. Maybe the difference was in how Paul disregarded authority. He didn't disregard authority for personal satisfaction. Rather, he saw a problem, and he disregarded everything that kept him from resolving it.

Benjamin Fuest had been a puzzle to Garik from their first meeting. The man had no clear skills, not any that were DNA enhanced. He would have expected him to have been assigned to Level 5 early on, but then Garik also had no overt and quantifiable skills, not like Jantzen, Justin, or Paolo, and he wasn't on Level 5.

Yet.

Fabiola Bella, while Garik hadn't known her long, she had a clear lack of interest in anyone who wasn't Fabiola. At least, that's the way Garik saw it, and he didn't think he was wrong.

He hadn't sorted out the Burgorski twins. Their ability to endlessly mimic any person or sound seemed like a useful trait, but both Anatoli and Andrey had used it to mock others. How could that be beneficial in a military sense?

When filling them in on what had happened since they'd been gone, Garik mentioned the power outage that had shut down the entire underground research center for two minutes, which brought grins, but most of all from Joanie. Garik asked why the happy faces and learned that was how Joanie had come so close to death. She and Alyna had stolen a military vehicle, and Tower security had pursued them. They'd driven it into the power transformer. It had blown, nearly killing Joanie but giving them the chance to escape. Her jellyfish DNA had triggered her body to revert to a younger self and begin regenerating. It was weeks before she woke and was able to function again. She still didn't have her full capabilities back, but she was getting stronger each day.

He also regaled them of some embarrassing things, such as Devon's daring dash to deliver Dieter to his dad at the hospital, and how he'd wound up in a crash and was now on crutches. John said he'd wondered about that. They had seen the video uploads showing the accident before they were taken down. They had no idea Garik was involved. Garik admitted it was his fault, and they wheedled him until he came clean. He'd wanted to keep Devon's tablet to search out what was happening in the city, but as it was, he was locked out anyway, so Devon had gotten injured for no reason, except to let Garik—who had been injured just as badly—know that he healed fast.

That got them onto Garik, asking what he had learned about himself, and had he developed any marked DNA-related skills, which set Garik to thinking. Some he shared, his hearing and sense of smell, and of course, healing amazingly fast, and he thought of his super speed and decided not to mention it. It was mostly useless, anyway, because it exhausted him, left him with quivering muscles and made him desperately hungry.

Precognition, they asked, like Christian? Garik said Rodheimer thought so, but he didn't see it. He just evaluated things cleanly, could anticipate, and didn't hesitate when in a tight situation. That wasn't precognition, just quick thinking.

Finally, Garik got around to Marisa, the one thing

he'd wanted to discuss more than anything else. He'd seen her one time, he'd thought, in a video in the Tower. His old friends were there, and a girl had been at the window wearing a shirt with his face on it.

They didn't know about that, but she had been instrumental in the shirts. After learning Garik wasn't deported, she'd contacted them through Garik's old friends, saying she wanted to fight the "system" and had gotten the students from Bay City High involved. That was much of what they'd been doing the past weeks, preparing the placards, setting up protest marches.

Garik pictured the destruction that had torn the city apart. "Surely there was an easier way. You've crippled Bay City."

"Not us," Justin growled. Once again, he didn't look up. He hadn't interacted much, just sat assembling an electronic kit, occasionally soldering and clicking switches to see if it worked yet.

"We were as surprised as anyone. People started showing up that we didn't know. We knew about the high school students, but the rest? They walked off buses from all over, taking up residence in the park and along street fronts. That's when the trouble started."

Garik thought of Kevin and his calls to get several fringe groups involved. What he said was, "So, the truck that took out the power station? An accident?"

"My idea." Joanie held up her hand hesitantly, but

she seemed proud. She said, "Hit 'em where it hurts."

"Alyna helped her steal the armored truck." John pantomimed her razorlike Komodo dragon claws. "Just," he went on, "copycats started stealing cars and running into everything. You must have driven past some of it. Which way did you come in?"

"Down Park," Justin growled. "I told you, John, I was overhead, tracking them, thinking it was Brace."

"Right." John snapped his fingers. "The Brace path. That's how he usually goes. I think he likes to see the destruction, part of the reason Justin was certain it was him, even though there were no support vehicles. You saw some of it then, cars left to burn out."

"And the one in the front of this building," Garik reminded them.

"That was me," Justin volunteered, still without looking up.

Paul had been dozing, and he sat up and said, "Did I get that right? You, Justin, have my utmost respect. You needed a hideout, and this was as good as any, but only if you could take out the surveillance systems first."

Justin didn't answer, but he did smile.

Garik took a deep breath and said, "Back to Marisa—"

Everyone stopped and looked at him, even Justin.

"No, my bushy-haired friend." John stood from the desk, and he walked across the room. "You cannot go see her." A small fridge served as the support underneath one end of a workstation. He pulled out a canned drink and popped the top. "I don't know why I don't save these for you people. I can cool my own."

"You're trying to distract me. Just stop it." Garik blew out his cheeks, and he tried to push his growing irritation to the back of his mind.

"Sure, let's talk about your girl," Justin said, his voice grating, the smile gone, his eyes down. "You like her so much, but does she feel the same? That's the question you must answer. Same as me and Jantzen, 'cept I know how Jantzen feels. He chose you."

Garik's face burned with anger then embarrassment. How could Justin say that about Marisa, and what he said about Jantzen? Too many things clicked in place, and that sent his thoughts reeling. He wanted to hit Justin, make him take his words back, but he knew it wouldn't be a fair fight. Marisa did care for him. She always had. They were best friends, always. No one could say different. And Jantzen had been a friend when he had no one else. He stood, paced in barely contained fury, then slammed his fist into a wall.

"You're a liar, Justin!" he spat.

Anger gets me nothing, he recited to himself, but it didn't help. In his fury, he had nothing but white hot in his head, and he was blinded to everything else. He hit the wall again, and fire encased his arm. He realized he'd smashed it so hard the first time, he must have broken bones in his hand. He staggered back and fell to his knees, clutching his hand to his chest.

"Hey, kid."

He looked up, his eyes leaking pain, with Justin over him. John and Joanie were in the background, and to the side, Paul flickered with amusement. He was enjoying this.

"I only asked if she felt the same. Must have hit a nerve, huh? I heard that hand crack the first time you hit the wall. The second time must have been murder. Stand up and let's see how fast you really heal."

The man pulled him to his feet, and he forced him to hold out his curled-up hand. Without warning, he opened the fist and pressed Garik's fingers flat.

"How's that?"

Garik couldn't answer. The expectation that it should hurt had scared him, and no words came out.

"Already healed, am I right? When we fought, I thought as much. We all heal fast, but not even they could have planned for you."

"You're an idiot." Garik jerked his hand away. "You goaded me just so I would do that."

"Goaded, yes. You hit the wall. I'd watch out if I were you." Justin returned to his electronic puzzle and took up the next piece.

"Watch out for what?" Garik looked to John and Joanie and to Paul. Paul shrugged.

"What, Justin?" He pushed on the man's shoulder,

determined he would look at him. Justin whipped his hands around and pinned Garik's arms.

"For what gets you angry. I've watched you. Those people in the Tower are smart. They've watched you, too. You've remained the same as when you first joined—"

"Kidnapped!"

"—and I expect that's about to change. Will the real Garik please stand up?" He released Garik and waved his arms in the air, making sure Garik took in the multiple joints. "I was the golden boy. I was *Jantzen's* golden boy, and then this happened. Something's going to be your trigger, and I think I know what it is. Chances, they do, too."

"Enough, Justin. Give the boy some space." John took Garik's shoulder and walked him away.

Trigger? What trigger? Garik sat, let his eyes find the hole in the wall, and asked himself, *What should I watch for? What makes me angry? And why should that make any difference?*

It would come to him. He was tired and hungry. Food would fix him for now, and tomorrow, he could figure out the rest.

And if he was still angry, maybe smash Justin in the face to remind him who was boss. That would sure feel good, and he suspected he wouldn't regret his decision afterwards.

In Book Seven, Garik Shayk faces his inner demon.

The Rage

Book Seven
The Human-Hybrid Project

Garik Shayk is free of the Tower's imprisonment for a second time. When his girlfriend, Marisa Bruni, is killed, he learns that anger is the key to triggering his non-human strength and uncanny ability to read a situation and act. Jantzen Hefferly breaks the news that only the Tower can help control his unbridled rage. Is returning to prison the answer? His decision may haunt Garik whichever he decides. The fractures in Garik's life started with the Tower, and if he returns, he is at their mercy once more.

The Human-Hybrid Project

Addictive!

A 10-book series you won't be able to forget. Explore each upcoming book, the characters, and more at www.thehumanhybridproject.com.

Book 1   Book 2

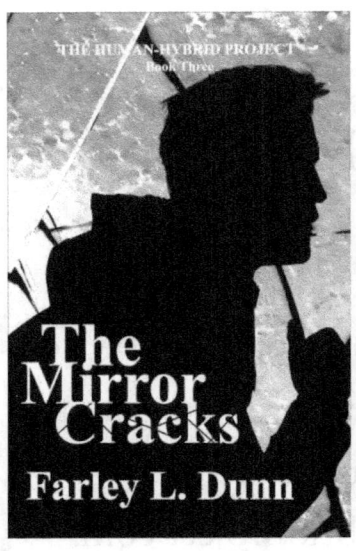

Book 3

Book 4

Book 5

Book 6

Book 7

Book 8

Book 9

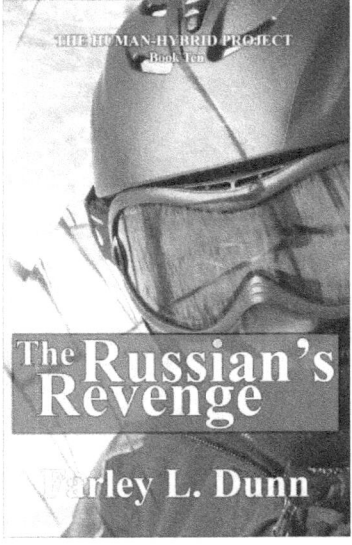

Book 10

www.ingramcontent.com/pod-product-compliance
Lightning Source LLC
Chambersburg PA
CBHW070559180626
46817CB00005B/1908